OUR SARNATH

JUDITH SONNET

Madness Heart Press
2006 Idlewilde Run Dr.
Austin, Texas 78744

Second Edition
ISBN: 978-1-967517-21-3
www.madnessheart.press

For

Jack, Calvin, and Morgan.

Thank you for letting me be a bother!

Praise for Judith Sonnet

"Judith is no one-note wonder, but an incredibly versatile author, specializing in vulnerable characters you can't help but relate to and want to protect." — Christine Morgan, author of *Lakehouse Infernal*.

"There are writers, but even rarer, there are storytellers. Judith Sonnet is a storyteller and of the very best kind: follow her down the path, unlatch the gate, and disappear inside the dark world she's cultivated. Once she takes you by the hand, you'll never look back." — Rebecca Rowland, author of *White Trash and Recycled Nightmares*.

"Judith Sonnet is so much more than an extreme horror writer. She knows how to write compelling, complex characters, and she knows what scares us." — Lucas Mangum, author of *Saint Sadist*.

"Welcome to my new favorite subgenre of horror: Judith Sonnet." —Gage Greenwood, author of *Bunker Dogs*.

"Judith Sonnet writes the kind of horror that sits with you long after you're finished, and her vast knowledge of horror's past shines through in just about everything she writes." —Duncan Ralston, author of *Ghostland*.

Part One
Beyond the Wall

Part Two
The Outsider

Part Three
The Dream Quest

PART ONE

BEYOND THE WALL

"But the sensitive are always with us, and sometimes a curious streak of fancy invades an obscure corner of the very hard-est of head; so that no amount of rationalization, reform, or Freudian analysis can quite annul the thrill of the chimney-corner whisper or the lonely wood."

H.P. Lovecraft, from his introduction to his essay "Supernatural Horror in Literature."

C H A P T E R   O N E

The cabin was smaller than Celeste Sessions expected.

When Theo had told her about it, he'd described it while stars glittered in his eyes, as if it was a home away from home. Homely, perhaps, was fitting, but this place did not look warm or welcoming. It was small and squat, with a porch overcrowded with pots, vases, cans, and tool boxes. She knew none of the rusted tools belonged to Theo, as he was a waiflike man with a gaunt face and soft hands. Probably, she thought, his brother, whose hands were like boxing gloves, who often hit Theo on the back hard enough to knock his teeth together and always asked when Theo was going to start working out so he could beat him in a fair fight. This always got a laugh from both men. At least Theo and his family were close, and both were intelligent . . . they just curved in opposite directions when it came to their areas of expertise and their physicality.

Celeste tried not to think of her own family, of her mother, but it couldn't be helped. She looked nervously at the journal sat on her lap, which she'd used to record her dreams over the previous seven days building up to the drive into the mountains—building up to tonight, when she was expected to have a dream so vivid and realistic, it would put these preliminary fantasies to shame.

I don't see it happening. These ones were pretty real. Pretty raw. Especially the one about Mom—

Theo was struggling to put on his jacket while sat behind the wheel. It'd been an hour's drive from Salt Lake City up into the mountains, and the snow had come down hard upon them. Constantly, Celeste was hypnotized by the *thwick-thwack* motions of the windshield wipers, which struggled to mitigate the snow. The landscape around them may have been overlayed with canvas and loose paper. So smooth, so pale, so white, it blotted out the textures of the mountain. Even its rumples were obscured, as snow filled in the crevices and crawled up the bases of tar-black, naked trees like an infestation of fuzzy, colorless mold.

In the hour it had taken for his truck (a sleek Ford pickup, which made Theo look misplaced when he was behind the wheel, like a child in his father's clothes) to travel to the cabin, he'd turned the heat up as high as it could go. Rapidly, both he and his partner had shed the heavier articles of clothing they'd stuffed themselves into before bringing their luggage out. Celeste's winter coat was coiled around her, bulging like an oversized belt. She'd rolled the arms of her sweater up, but that, too, eventually had to come off and was now trapped between her thighs, one sleeve dangling toward the floorboard. Her earmuffs sat around her neck, and her cap was on the top of the dashboard, where it had threatened to fall the higher up the mountain they climbed.

She put her dream journal down on the floor and followed Theo's lead, throwing her sweater over her head and wrestling it around the obstructing earmuffs she could have easily removed beforehand yet chose not to. When she was bundled up, she was breaking a sweat, but that was cured when she propped her door open. The wind blasted into the interior of Theo's Ford, filling up the once tropical atmosphere with arctic cruelty.

Her hands got the worst of it first. She dug around the pockets of her jacket until she found her mittens (they'd been a birthday gift from a friend, even though Celeste had been born in July, but her friend knew her well and always got her what she needed rather than what she wanted. They were the only reason Celeste had snowshoes too, for which Celeste was doubly thankful. She and Theo both were academics, and the stereotype rang true they could be absentminded). She fit the left mitten on quickly before the right, then she scooped her journal back up and held it defensively, like a teddy bear against her chest. She couldn't stand to be apart from it for very long, and she figured that was a resuscitation of childhood paranoia. She'd always been a nervous kid, and a lot of those old nervous thoughts had been brought screaming back via her dreams.

Don't think about those yet, a cautious voice said in her head. The same voice that reminded her to look both ways before crossing the road or told her to check the expiration date on her milk before pouring it on her cereal. It was the voice of reason, of patience. It wasn't a voice she always listened to, but when she did, she always thought she ought to take heed of it more often. *You and Theo will be talking enough about dreams in a few hours. This is the first night of the ritual, and he said it will prove to you that all of it is real.*

Does he need to prove it? Celeste wondered. *I think I already believe.*

"Brrr," she said aloud, insistently, holding herself and shaking like she was on stage and she wanted the people in the nosebleeds to feel the cold for themselves.

Theo snorted and wove his scarf around the lower part of his face. He lowered it so he could speak without muffling his voice, but the scarf stayed up around his cheeks, keeping them concealed. She didn't have to look in a mirror to know her own skin had been beaten red by the sharp winds. Scarves and thick coats were necessary this high in the mountains, even when it was warm in the city.

"What possessed you to even come out here?" Theo asked.

"You did. You and your crazy ideas," she said offhandedly.

"Damn right, I did," Theo said before propping his own door open and letting one foot hang out of the vehicle. "You want the key? You can get the door open and the heat going, and I'll get as much of the luggage as I can."

"Yes. Yes. Yes. Yes." She held out a mittened

hand and beckoned.

He turned the key and removed it from the ignition. The heater could do them no favors anyways with the doors open. She snatched it quickly, hopped out of the car, and then trudged up the path and toward the front of the Theobald family cabin, where her lover had told her he'd spent every Christmas since he was a baby, and where, next month, the Theobald family would spend yet another Christmas. Perhaps (she hoped) she'd be there too.

Things were getting serious with the eldest of the Theobald brood. She'd only met his brother, Richmond Theobald Jr., and that was because she'd worked with Rich and he'd taken her out first. The date had been pleasant, but they'd discovered they made better friends than companions within minutes. On the way home, he'd told her that he thought she'd like his older brother. He was smart, well read, and he was interested in all the same "new age stuff you like."

"What's his name?" she'd asked.

"Theo."

"Theo Theobald?"

"No. Sorry. He prefers Theo. His first name is Louis, and he hates it. I'm surprised he hasn't had it legally changed. Maybe he's waiting for our folks to die before he does." Rich bark-laughed.

"It's an annoying process," Celeste said.

"Oh, yeah. I didn't even think about that," Rich said, silently acknowledging he knew Celeste was a trans woman. It was the first time the topic had been brought up that night, and it felt covert. Celeste was open about who she was, but she didn't always feel the need to state it outright, especially when she was with people like Rich, who was grounded, had eyes, and didn't seem to require coddling and hand-holding. He was a good man, Theo's brother, but when she met Theo, she knew right away Rich was also a smart one.

Because Theo and Celeste were instantly attracted to each other, instantly stimulated by their various points of interest, instantly relieved by their similarities and their differences. Was it love at first sight? No. But it was . . . something. All Rich had to do was make introductions, step back, watch the fireworks, then mosey on to the bar, where he struck up a fast conversation with a group of strangers who he now (five months later) played squash with.

The Theobald brothers both had big personalities, but they were honed toward different skills. Rich was athletic, down-to-earth, and financially savvy. He drove a new car every two years and lived in a three-story house in the suburbs. He was a professor of mathematics, which was how he knew Celeste, who taught Western Literature, but most of his money came from his connections in the tech industry (a world so foreign to a luddite like Celeste, it may have been Xanadu or Atlantis), where he used his skills to help program financing apps.

Theo, on the other hand, was closer to Celeste's speed. He didn't have a Facebook account, and he wrote poorly reviewed fiction. He lived in an apartment in downtown Salt Lake City, which he shared with a much younger roommate. Theo was thirty-five, and his roommate, a twenty-two-year-old, had found him through a craigslist ad Rich had made for him. They barely spoke, only sharing time in the living room to watch TV because they both saw eye-to-eye when it came to cooking competition shows (the louder the chefs yelled, the better the show).

He was practical, deliberate, and habitual, Theo was. Every morning, he awoke at five on the dot. His showers were exactly six minutes long. He counted his brush strokes while he worked on his immaculately white teeth. He combed his brown, slightly-long hair carefully, as if he was afraid it would all unravel if he pulled too hard. Sometimes, after she'd stayed over, Celeste would sit on the closed toilet lid and watch him work, fascinated by the way time and Earth seemed to stop around him just so he could complete one task at a time, being sure to get it right each time. She wished she could be so focused, but Celeste had always been flighty. When she was a child, she'd sometimes walk into walls when her thoughts left her head and floated up into the ether, far away from where she was on Earth. She always slept in (even when she set multiple alarms), and she usually rushed out the door with tangles in her hair and one sleeve caught on her elbow while the other fell around her wrist.

He didn't seem annoyed by their differences. Maybe growing up with Rich (who was a proud rough-houser) had prepared him to accept others for who they were. But also, Theo skipped out on the ego most academics and writers were purported to have. He didn't want to fit the world (or other people) into his own image. He just cared about his own image, and he took care of it as best he could, maintaining it the way a thoughtful older man does the car he used to cruise in. Theo's apartment was so clean it was sterile, his hairs never fell astray, and his nails were dutifully clipped and groomed, even better than her own, which she painted brightly sometimes to mask their rough edges.

"Why doesn't Theo teach?" she'd asked Rich over a friendly night of drinks with some colleagues from the university.

Rich hesitated, holding his frothy beer up to his bearded face. She couldn't help but wonder if he was trying to obscure an errant expression. Something that could give away more than he wanted to. "He hasn't told you?"

"No."

"He used to. He got blacklisted. I guess he doesn't like talking about it."

"Blacklisted?" She was genuinely shocked. "Don't tell me he did something horrible, Rich."

"No. Nothing like that. Theo just has some crazy ideas. Or . . . had. He calmed down as he grew up. In high school, he was convinced aliens were real. He caught pneumonia after sneaking out of the house to sit in a field for an entire night, waiting for starships. It sounds even crazier than it was when I say it out loud. He's just always been . . . you know. He's creative. He's an artist. Most of them either go crazy or had a crazy phase. For Theo, it was just a phase. It lasted a while, but it was just a phase. Afterwards, he got sorted, and now he's on track. You see his morning routine yet?"

She blushed a little. "Yes."

"That's what he was missing. Discipline." He winked. "And a good woman."

"You sound like an old film character sometimes, you know? Like Sam Elliott in *The Quick and the Dead.*"

"He called Kate Capshaw a 'mighty handsome woman,' didn't he?"

"A 'fine' one too."

"She is. Has she done anything recently, or is she retired? Hell, if I married Spielberg and could afford to retire, I would. Anyways, sarcasm veils honesty. Theo won't stop talking about you."

It was only the next morning when Celeste realized Rich hadn't answered the initial question. What had Theo done that had gotten him blacklisted from teaching? Rich had assuaged her fears but had not clarified the reality of the situation. She decided to ask Theo outright, thinking that had perhaps been Rich's intention. It might not have been his story to completely tell, and so he'd navigated around it as best he could.

The weekend after her conversation with Rich, she and Theo met up for coffee in Sugarhouse, where they sometimes liked to go to read. They could enjoy each other's company without even speaking, just lost in their individual books and thoughts. It was another sign that the relationship was going smoothly. Most men she'd been with previously had felt the need to fill the air with words, even when the air was perfectly fine to breathe as it was. Conversational garnish had become an irritant, especially after a long week of work, and sometimes, she just wanted to be around someone she cared about without having to perform for them or watch them put on a show themselves.

She broached the subject gently and was pleased when Theo wasn't shocked or offended by the inquiry. They were drinking lattes on the back porch, occasionally looking up from their books to watch the sunset or the occasional frazzled college student who they may or may not have recognized.

"I should have told you before, but it is an embarrassing story. I'm glad Rich brought it up, though, or I might have procrastinated myself into not talking about it at all. Really, I am sorry." He set his coffee cup down and ran his hand over the surface of his closed book, a leatherbound tome called *Eibon*, which had no author and was reported to be incredibly rare, which made Celeste nervous, since Theo touched it with his bare hands and seemed to tug the pages whenever he turned them. He'd laughed her concerns away, saying, "This book has seen far worse than me." He was always reading old manuscripts. She'd never seen him even consider a book written in the 20th century. He particularly enjoyed works on alchemy, obscure philosophy, and ancient religious practices. He said they inspired his own books much more than Stephen King or Frank Herbert ever could. He also didn't watch movies (even the old ones), as he claimed they polluted the imagination. Celeste was almost thankful their interests diverged here. The last thing she wanted was a partner who was an expert in her own field. She'd once dated a literary professor, and he'd become rapidly insufferable after she stated she thought John Updike's *Couples* was the great American novel and any accusations that his works were masturbatory missed the point of literature in general. All of it, she thought, was masturbatory. Melville, Hemmingway, Steinbeck, up to the more modern American writers, like John Irving and Richard Yates. Even Cormac McCarthy, whose merit she thought would someday be comparable to Faulkner's.

If you discredited the works of self-important men who felt they had something to say that everyone must listen to . . . then you would be discrediting not just modern literature but *all* literature.

Well, Theo did discredit it. Not because he hated it, or because he thought himself above it, or because he had a misguided counterargument . . . but simply because it was not what he was interested in.

What he cared about, and she knew this by the passion that flared his nostrils whenever it was discussed, was old religion. There were, he said, a plethora of myths, practices, and stories that had been largely and unfairly forgotten to time. Cultures and languages which could not be translated but should be studied. He said what he read was like holding the plug of a life support system into the wall just before it fell out. He was keeping, in his own way, long-deserted people alive, while the rest of the world had moved on without them.

She thought sometimes he ought to have become an archeologist, seeking a Rosetta Stone for villages and temples that had come and been paved quickly over by more popular cultures. Sometimes, he discussed half-mulched fragments of ancient tablets like they were revolutionary, and to him, they were . . . because they gave hints to the more undiscovered portions of human history.

"I mean, think of it in modern terms . . . There are so many *things* happening right now, a person would go crazy trying to keep track of it all. It's impossible. We like to think of history as a straight line. The fifties were all milkshakes and crooners. The sixties were all protests and hippies. The seventies were all about peace and free sex. The eighties were all neon ads and brown furniture. But you know that's an oversimplification. What about today? The cultures and communities and theories and religions and conspiracies and works that are there one second and gone the next. Will anyone remember them in fifty years? What will happen in three hundred years when digital archeologists dig through an old hard drive and discover someone's art they never shared? Will they become the Van Gogh of our time, long after our time is past? That's what I care about. The personal touch of people who don't even know I now know a piece of their selves. A god that could have become the world's religion but was suppressed and stamped out before its worshippers could become organized."

He'd explained it before, and she'd held his every word with fascination. She shared her loves as well, and he listened intently, understanding her love and passion the way she did his. But now, he was going to explain why this passion had not translated into a career, how he'd lost his opportunity to impress upon others the importance of what he studied.

"I started to believe in it," Theo stated bluntly, running his fingers over the cover of his old book, looking beyond her and toward the parking lot, where a group of kids with dyed hair and piercings smoked cigarettes and talked confidently and loudly about what they would do to solve the conflict in the Middle East. She'd been trying all evening not to let their conversation interfere with her concentration, and it was still a struggle, even as Theo told her something that showed (for the first time since they'd started seeing each other) how vulnerable he could be. She realized the memory was making him misty-eyed, that he was trying to find the right words.

"What do you mean?" she asked.

"I was teaching at a small private school. I'd done well in school myself and was young, dumb, and ready to take the world by the horns. I was also obsessive. At that point in my life, I had a mentor who had a collection of rare and obscure Bibles."

"Bibles?"

"Not Christian ones. Bibles for old religions. Some of her books were untranslatable, but we read through them anyways, making guesses. Some of the books . . . she'd translated herself. She built a codex for each one, and even with all our hard work and effort, we could only scratch at the surface of what those works contained. It was time-consuming and exhausting. I started to spend every day at her house, in her library, working myself thin. I skipped meals, I missed birthdays and holidays, and my lessons . . . changed. I was being worn down by her, which was, perhaps, the point. But I entered this state willingly. No one had ever validated my interests before. There's no section in theology class about the city of Ib or the god its people worshipped, or the weirder, lesser gods of Egyptian mythology, or the sea gods which were worshipped on the American coast when we had only begun to colonize this country—and she knew it. The information she gave me was intoxicating, Celeste. I spent every day there, studying, reading books I couldn't actually read. Eventually, my mind began to make sense of the senseless. I was convinced I'd exposed myself to so much of it, opened myself up to so much of it, I was being given the gift of second sight. I thought I could read these ancient scrolls and scriptures the way a piano prodigy can read the keys without knowing a single note. I went crazy, writing out my own English versions of these books." He had to catch his breath.

"What happened next?" Celeste asked.

"She encouraged it. When I brought her a made-up religious ritual I'd scrawled out, we practiced it . . . convinced ourselves it worked. That all the forgotten religions were true. We saw stars and gods and demons and angels, and we saw them together, so we could confirm to ourselves what we were seeing was real."

"But they weren't?"

He shuddered. "I had a breakdown at school. In the middle of it, I tried to teach my students how to perform a blood rite. I was sent to a hospital and stayed there for the better part of a year. When I returned, I'd been replaced and blacklisted. The school had barely managed to keep quiet what I'd done, and they wanted nothing more to do with me. My 'mentor' abandoned me. She vanished into the night, taking her library with her." He paused. "She was named Lavinia Carter Whateley, and she'd been my friend when I was younger. We lived on the same block, and my parents thought it was nice I spent so much time with an older woman when I was a teenager, helping around her house, listening to her stories, learning from her. They didn't know what she was teaching me. If they'd known, they would have put a stop to it. But I was young. I didn't know it was wrong. I grew up thinking it was fine, that I wasn't being—well, I don't even like to say it. I'm sorry." Theo shuddered deeply.

Celeste decided not to probe this issue further, but she squeezed his hand reassuringly, as if to tell him he didn't need to tell her what he wasn't ready to share, but she understood, or at least could try to understand, the hurt he'd been dealt.

"I grew up thinking she was the smartest person on the planet. She wasn't. She just took advantage of a young boy who wanted guidance, and she turned him into a very damaged man. When I had my breakdown, when I went to the hospital, I was seeing monsters and demons every time I opened my eyes. It took some time to unwind the spell she'd put me under." Theo sighed. "I'm sorry if this is heavy."

"No. Please, I wanted to know."

"Well, after that, I decided even if I could somehow find my way into a teaching position again, I didn't want it. What I wanted was to reclaim what I loved. I felt like it had been tainted by Lavinia, and so I decided to take it back from her. It took a long time, but it was worth it. Then I began writing, making my own stories out of the things I learned. I found when I put them in a fictional story, in a book, they didn't have the same power over me. It may not have led me to fame and fortune, like I wanted when I was younger, but it made me happy, and it put my knowledge to good use. Sometimes, I hope Lavinia is reading my work, angry that I've taken what she did to me and made something new out of it. Sometimes, I hope she's forgotten who I am. Sometimes, I hope she died in a car accident, and no one showed up to her funeral, and all her books were donated to a small library where they're hardly read."

One of the teenagers laughed loudly, almost breaking Celeste out of an illusion she hadn't realized she'd envisioned; that she and Theo were the only people on Earth, that they were totally isolated on the back porch of the café, and if there were any other people left around them, they couldn't see or hear the couple. They were ghosts, wafting together, entangling their spirits into one haunting that looked something like a will-o'-the-wisp. The illusion was shattered, but that it had even existed was beautiful enough.

"That's the other side of the coin. Because sometimes . . . some things deserve to be forgotten. Some religions are terrible. Some writers are shitty. Some men called themselves philosophers when they were actually thoughtless con artists. Some art is ugly. Some books are supposed to gather dust. I won't deny them their right to exist, but unlike Lavinia . . . I don't think every god deserves to be worshiped."

Later, while he slept beside her, Celeste set her hand on his chest and felt his heartbeat. She hadn't known he'd gone through so much in his childhood, and she admired his bravery, sharing that part of him with her. She wondered when she'd be brave enough to do the same.

Celeste had also been abused when she was young. Not by a neighbor, but by her mother. A harsh woman who was convinced she could turn her daughter back into a son. It had been a grueling adolescence, filled with arguments, with beatings, with scrutiny. Every step Celeste took had been harshly criticized, and every plea for understanding had met deaf ears. And then, the day Celeste left for good, her mother had come into her room late one night with a knife—

She pinched her eyes closed, not wanting to remember it. That night haunted her, and she thought it always would. Despite the therapy, the healing, and the acceptance she'd found among her peers in Salt Lake City, she always worried, just before she closed her eyes, if she'd dream of that madwoman she'd once loved coming into her room with determined eyes, the knife dripping out of her fist like an icicle off the corner of their roof. She'd left a memento too, a moon-shaped scar on Celeste's left palm. She'd raised her hand to defend herself, and the knife had slashed it.

I'll tell him. When I'm ready.

And maybe she'd tell him today, she thought as she stomped through the snow and toward the cabin, clutching her journal close, her teeth chattering as the wind zapped her like a Martian beam. Up the steps and onto the porch, she hurried to pull the keys Theo had tossed her out of her pocket. The mittens made her hands clumsy, but she managed to fit the key into the lock and turn it. The door opened so easily, she wondered if it had even been locked in the first place. A small spark of panic dinged off her ribcage as she considered a horror movie possibility.

What if some mad drifter had come by, broken in, and was now lurking in the house, clutching a fragmented bottle or a garden trowel? She pushed the paranoia away and trudged inside, stomping her feet on the welcome mat. Chunks of white snow fell off her boots like volcanic ash. The inside of the cabin was just as cold as the outside.

She hurried in, looking for the climate control system. Thankfully, they wouldn't have to rely only on the fireplace to warm their hands here, but the fire was going to help.

She took her boots off quickly, leaving them beside the door, where they developed pools. Her feet were freezing cold as she padded around the cabin in search of heat. Just as she was about to give up and put some dry logs in the fireplace, she spotted the dial next to the pantry door.

After putting it on high heat (the Theobalds could afford it, she argued, and it wasn't like they'd keep it up the whole week), she surveyed the area. The cabin was much nicer on the inside than it was on the overcrowded and weathered porch. The chimney was built in the very middle of the house, with one half being a high-ceiling living room and then the other having an almost secretive staircase that led up to the master bedroom, which had a wall that divided it from what might have been an office space but had become an improvised third bedroom, with a military-style cot squeezed between the space where the roof slanted into a knee-high wall. It was the sort of bed you didn't sleep well on, and if you woke up too fast, you risked knocking your noggin on the ceiling.

The master bedroom was the second biggest room in the house. The bed was cozy, but it had been long neglected. A small layer of fuzzy dust rested on the warm quilt, and the pillows looked stiff. Celeste decided she'd do a load of laundry before they settled down for the night.

The bed faced a picturesque window, but with all the snow coming down, it might have been covered in wet newspaper. If they were here in the summer, Celeste could imagine a hot beam of sunlight streaming in, landing on the bed, and rousing its sleepers better and kinder than any alarm clock. As always when Celeste went on vacation to remote places, she wondered what it would be like to drop everything and live on the land. She assumed she'd take to gardening, even though she'd never done it before.

The only other item of note within the bedroom was an oaken writing desk, which sat beside the window. A fountain pen stood erect next to a hardbacked dictionary and a well-loved thesaurus. All these, she realized, belonged to Theo. He'd told her sometimes he came out here on his own just to write.

The living room came with two couches, which sat in an L shape against the walls opposite the dining table. There was a liquor cabinet (it was stocked, thank God), a coffee table, and a thick rug that warmed her aching feet. In the weird nether-space between the living and dining areas, there was a sliding glass door, which opened onto the back porch. The porch was almost buried in snow, and the yard was a blank slate. She'd seen a picture before of Theo in the backyard, so she knew there was a pleasant walking path which led toward the creek and a tree house, which the boys had played "soldiers" in when they were young. The tree house was in disrepair, Theo had told her, and looked more like a deer stand. She tried to see it, but the snow was obscuring the finer details. It almost hurt to look through; there was just so much of it.

A secondary bedroom was located right beside the front door, and on its opposite was the bathroom/laundry room, which Celeste was happy to see came with a shower.

By the time she was in the kitchen, opening drawers and acclimating herself to where the utensils were, Theo came into the cabin, lugging two suitcases in his gloved hands while a third was pinned between his arm and ribcage.

"Oh, let me help!" She started toward him.

Theo smiled and shook his head. "I've got it, but maybe you can grab the door behind me?"

She squeezed against the hallway wall to let him by, then snapped the door closed. The welcome mat was soaked now with the snow they'd brought in. Then she realized Theo was still wearing his boots and had tracked a path from the door to the living room. Thankfully, the floors were all hardwood, so that would be an easy fix. Still, he came back hurriedly, boots in hand, and he tried not to laugh as he set them beside hers. "If Mom was here, she'd throw a fit."

"I want to start unpacking. We are sleeping upstairs, right?"

"Where else?" He cocked a thumb to the door by his side. "Lord knows what Rich does in there when we aren't looking."

"Is your parent's bed any better?"

Theo covered his ears. "I can't hear you. I can't hear you. I can't hear you."

They brought their luggage upstairs, choosing which sides of the bed they wanted before Theo suddenly grabbed her by the waist, pulled her near, and planted a tender kiss on her cold lips. When they separated, she raised her brows.

"What's that for?"

"Warmth. I'm freezing." His hands squeezed her hips and kept her close. "I've been thinking of kissing you all day."

"Then kiss me again."

He did. Outside, the wind brayed as they stood together in the cabin, swaying gently as if under the influence of a secret, invisible breeze. She closed her eyes, shutting down everything except for his hands and lips. The way he touched her, the way he held her, the way their tongues darted toward each other, only to slink away, knowing a little restraint would go a long way to ensuring a better time when night fell.

When they finally separated, he cupped her cheek and seemed to study her face, a habit of his she never tired of. As if he was trying to take a snapshot without a camera, or he was a painter who was beginning to feel inspired. The twinkle in his eyes lit up his pale, narrow face.

"You're beautiful. Do you know that?"

She put her hand over his, squeezing it between her palm and cheek so he could feel her smile as well as see it.

"Thank you . . . for doing this. I know it's a lot to ask, but it's . . ." His voice trailed off. "Hey. Are you hungry?"

"Starving."

"I'll fetch the cooler."

They kissed again, then parted.

While Theo braved the elements, Celeste unpacked their clothing and filed them neatly into the closet and the dresser-drawers. She wished she could take credit for the folded clothing, but this was all Theo's work. He had packed his bag carefully and deliberately, like he was working retail and there was a strict code that needed following, while Celeste had stuffed hers chaotically, rolling some of her sweaters into balls before shoving them into the bulging bag.

After the bags were empty and she'd retrieved their separate toiletry cases and brought them down to the bathroom, Celeste found Theo halfway through the cooler, organizing the food they'd brought into the vacant fridge.

"You want to warm up with a drink?" he asked.

"Not on an empty stomach," she replied.

"Well, I think I'll make dinner tonight."

"I'll do the dishes."

"You don't have to—"

"I want to. What are you cooking?"

"Salmon on rice with veggies, or spaghetti and meatballs?"

"Meatballs. We'll save the fancy stuff for later."

"I think I forgot the peas. Damn—wait, here they are."

"Do you want a drink?"

"A little one. Whiskey. Neat."

"On it."

She changed her mind and poured herself one. In the kitchen, while he got a pot of water boiling, they tapped glasses, set them against the counter quickly, lifted them back up, and silently gulped their whiskey down. The alcohol burned all the way into the pit of Celeste's stomach.

"Another?"

"I'll wait," he said.

Dinner ended up being spaghetti with meatballs, a side of peas and carrots, and fresh garlic bread. Theo was a fine cook, and Celeste was pleased. They ate voraciously, lost in their meals, narrated by the howling of the wind. It wasn't until they were each on their second plate that they conversated.

"This place is really nice. You were right."

"Did you think I was lying?" Theo said after slurping up a noodle and covering his mouth with a polite hand. He always ate like he should be ashamed of it, hunched slightly, hiding his face even though she knew he chewed with his mouth tightly shut.

"People always talk up their cabins," she replied, spearing a meatball and lifting it.

"How many have you stayed at?"

"My friends and I have gone to a few too many bachelorette parties."

"What happens in Vegas . . ."

"I'm so sick of male strippers."

He chuckled softly. "So, would you like to talk about your dreams soon?"

The sudden shift was jarring. "Maybe not over dinner," she said.

He blushed a bit. "Sorry. I just thought of it. Been so busy today—"

"No, it's fine. I'm looking forward to it. I just . . . I want to focus on it when we get to it."

She'd left the journal upstairs on top of their bed, half hoping they'd save it for tomorrow, even though she knew that was impossible. He'd already told her the ritual had to begin the night they arrived, which is why they'd left late, so both of them could sleep in before staying up for half the night.

"It *does* work," he said. "It's the only one that did."

Theo raised his hands. "I won't say anything else. We'll talk later."

"Okay," she relented, looking at the meatball like it might comfort her. She put it in her mouth and chewed leisurely, wondering, not for the first time (or last), why she'd agreed to this.

Because you love him. You're sure of it now, a sturdy voice said to her. *You were sure of it a few weeks after you started seeing him, and you both are close to saying it. It's been a long time coming, but he said he needed time. He needed to be sure.*

I think he's sure. I can see it just behind his eyes, lurking there. Love. Actual love. He's just scared of it. And I don't blame him. After everything that happened, everything she *did to him* (she didn't even like thinking of Lavinia's name), *I have to be patient and understanding. And isn't this the true test of both qualities?*

The one ritual he still believes in. The Dream Cycle. The one he claimed still worked, even after he'd been "deprogramed" from his abuser's manipulative nonsense. The ritual he said had helped aid his recovery, and one he'd claimed stoutly and obstinately for himself.

It seemed a little crazy at first when he told me about it, but after the last seven days . . . after the dreams I've had . . . maybe I'm starting to believe too.

Now there was a scary thought.

She swallowed more than her food, then squirmed in her seat. "I guess I can't avoid it now, can I?"

"Sorry I jumped the gun. I'm just excited. And nervous," he said.

"No need to apologize." She tilted forward. "If I didn't write them down, would I have forgotten the dreams?"

He shook his head. "No. The finer details, sure, but not the way they feel. Every time I've done it, the dreams have always been . . . real. Before and after."

"If they weren't, maybe I would have tried to talk us out of it this weekend," she admitted. "Maybe I still will. It's scary."

"At first, but then it becomes . . . you'll see. It's special." He smirked. "Did I tell you Rich knows about it?"

"He does?"

"He says I deserve a little bit of craziness so long as the big stuff doesn't come back." He laughed in a way that was supposed to sound offhanded but came off nervous. "I tried to get him to come out here and try it, but he didn't want to. If you don't want to, we'll stop. You don't have to do this, Celeste, but it means a lot that you wanted to try."

She pondered for a second, wondering if she oughtn't take the out since it was being so graciously offered. They could spend the weekend just talking, making love, looking out at the snowy wonderland that surrounded them while they drank hot coffee and read the books she'd packed with her. She didn't have to perform a magic ritual to finally open up to him about her mother. They could simply sit across from each other and have a real, adult conversation about it.

But she was curious. She was excited. She wanted to understand the man she'd fallen in love with in totality, and if she changed course now, if they didn't go through with it, she could only guess at this part of him. This important part of him, which he insisted had saved his life and sanity. This ritual which was, to him, as important as prayer, as Sunday worship, was to those who were convinced they were destined for Heaven.

Celeste didn't want to miss out on this part of Theo, even if it scared her, even if it was strange. But she was strange herself, wasn't she? And she'd wanted understanding when she'd first come out of the closet and hadn't found it. How unfair would it therefore be if she didn't at least try to understand him? If she denied him an opportunity to share who he was just so she could be more comfortable?

"No," she said. "I want to do it. I want to try. After dinner, I'm going to get my journal, okay? We'll get right into it immediately, and I'll do the dishes in the morning."

He smiled, then covered his mouth with one hand while lifting his fork with the other. Silently, they finished their meal, and then Celeste went upstairs. She came back down slowly, as if she was ill-prepared to make a speech in front of a crowded concert hall and wanted to put the big moment off with each footstep.

When she came into the living room, she found the cabin empty.

Minutes passed before the front door reopened and

Theo came back in, shivering from the cold. He was carrying the black doctor's bag he'd almost stealthily put in the car before they'd left Salt Lake City. It was sleek and polished, looking brand new even though he'd told her it was an antique when she'd first discovered it under his bed while looking for a lost sweater. She knew the contents, as he'd already opened the bag for her once and showed her what was inside, telling her it was the only thing Lavinia had ever given him he'd chosen to keep, and each item was fundamental to the Dream Cycle.

I should have told you about this before, but I didn't know how.

It's the one thing I still believe in.

I believe in it because it works.

Because it works.

It works.

He took off his boots, then brought the bag into the living room. He set it down on the coffee table with caution, as if there was a litter of wet kittens inside it. Leaving it closed, he went to the fireplace and stacked logs inside it, filling the gaps with crinkled newspaper. The fire caught quickly and spread its heat through the living room, which gave Theo an excuse to finally turn the heater off. While he worked, Celeste's eyes were drawn to the bag. It was heavier than Theo made it look, she knew. Lifting it initially, she'd thought it had a bowling ball in it before she realized the shape wasn't right.

Theo sat down beside her on the couch. Together,

they shared a moment's silence before he leaned forward, plucked the bag up, and set it on his lap.

"Tell me about your dreams," he said, his voice cool and steady. "And I'll tell you mine."

CHAPTER TWO

Celeste opened her journal. She'd scrawled the first one out in a hurry.

"This was Friday, after I'd agreed to come out this weekend," she told him. "That night, I struggled to get to sleep. I was overthinking . . . and I missed you. I know you said we shouldn't sleep together before leaving, but I had gotten accustomed to having you around, and my bed just felt so . . . empty. So I didn't fall asleep until midnight, and when I did, I didn't sleep long. The dream came at me suddenly and woke me with a start, and I wrote it down by moonlight, so it's the least detailed of all of them." She cleared her throat.

I awoke to find myself in a graveyard. It looked like a theater set with a fog machine and Styrofoam tombstones, each one more crooked than the last. I walked through the fog, shaking in the cold. I felt like I had eyes on me. I awoke when something rose up from the fog ahead of me. It was shaped like a man, but I somehow understood it wasn't one. It was something that had been buried deeper than the bodies in the graves, and it was coming up just to see me.

When she finished, Theo broke the bag open. A humid smell rose into the air, polluting it. He pulled out a ratty journal that fit in his palm and handed it to her. "You'll see the date by the first entry," he said.

She read it quickly, frowning as she did.

I dreamed tonight of a graveyard. A place that was both real and false, like a simulation of a cemetery, constructed by an artist who'd only read of such places in books. It must be, I thought, what a time traveler from the dark ages would make of our modern renaissance fairs. I stumbled through the graves, feeling drunk as I inhaled the seedy odor of the dirt and the tart fog that blanketed me. Up ahead, I spotted a ghostly specter, and the sight of it startled me awake before I could take in any of the finer details. I do know there was something misshapen about the figure. Like he was deformed, or like his body was man-shaped but not exactly manlike.

"And you know I haven't looked at your journal before today, right?"

"Yeah. I've kept it under lock and key at home," Celeste said. "Besides, you can't fake this. The paper is aged and the words are faint."

"The rest are different, but the first dream is always the same . . . for everyone. There's the graveyard and the thing in it, and then the sudden waking. Every time I've done this, the dream always comes back exactly how I remembered it. I'm almost so familiar with it now, it comforts me."

She read the date. This was the first time he and Lavinia had performed the rite, back when he was a teenager. Long before his breakdown, before his hospital stay, before Lavinia had vanished permanently from his life (*Which had been*, she thought, *the least Lavinia could have done to make right all the wrongs she'd done to him*).

It was genuine. They'd had the exact same dream. It didn't remove all the doubt from Celeste's mind, but it removed a chunk of it. Like a glacial wall, it slipped away and dissolved.

"Can you explain that?" Theo asked as Celeste handed back his journal.

"No," Celeste said.

"I just wanted you to see it yourself," he continued.

Not sure what to say, Celeste picked her own journal back up and narrowed her eyes. "The second night, the dream was longer. I expected to be returned to the graveyard, but it was different in every single way . . . and it wasn't scary." Again, she cleared her throat before reading.

I dreamed I'd just stepped out of a greenhouse and found myself in a long, green meadow. I wanted to turn and see the greenhouse behind me, but I could not. My eyes and body were intent on moving forward, taking me across the meadow and toward the woods beyond. The air was still and calm, and the sun was shielded just enough so it could warm me without blinding me. In the distance, I heard horses. They came toward the meadow, breaking through the woods. Three of them. I saw three men riding atop the animals, each one wearing a golden crown and a long beard. They saw me and began to ride happily toward me, shouting my name. The dream then seemed to cut, as dreams do, a few hours ahead. We were sitting together on the meadow, the horses grazing nearby, a picnic blanket spread around us and stacked with succulent foods. The main course was a giant bird of some sort, larger yet leaner than a turkey. Its feet were intact, hooked into agonized claws. There was something I did not like about the meal, and I did not eat it. Meanwhile, my three kings were devouring the bird as if they'd been fasting. Chunks of meat dropped from their mouths as they followed each bite with a hearty swig of wine. It was as if they were mistaken and believed we were in the midst of a party rather than a quaint picnic. I couldn't help but laugh at them, which they didn't notice (and if they did, they did not care). They ate hastily, pushing as much food in their faces as they could, their magnificent beards streaked with red wine and chunks of white meat. Their faces looked like filthy birds' nests. Then, to my surprise, one of the kings removed his crown, stood, and began to walk away, leaving me with the other two. I asked the king with the red beard where his friend was going. He spoke around a mouthful, telling me that this king was allowed to leave, while he and his friend were not. This king, he said, had changed his ways. I was unsure what he meant, and I woke up puzzled.

"Interesting," Theo said. "I believe there's something to that one. Typically, the dreams are not quite so revealing so fast. They tend to build up to it."

"Revealing of what? I still don't understand it," Celeste said.

"It has to do with the history of the ritual," Theo said. "Maybe. I think it's best we leave it without my interpretations. I wouldn't want to influence your dreams tonight anyways."

She sighed. "I was kind of hoping you'd just tell me. The rest of the dreams made sense to me, actually. This is the one that left me stumped."

"We'll talk about it later . . . but I want to know about your third dream. What happened next?"

"The next night was easier still, which I'm thankful for. The previous two nights gave me a lot to chew on, and I was pretty surprised I went to sleep so quickly. But I dreamed I was floating in space. I've had dreams like that before, you know? Where everything is dark. But unlike those dreams, time moved the same. I was just suspended in darkness, not scared, not particularly feeling anything at all. It felt more like I was being prepared for something, like they were giving me a rest before they gave me something really . . . well . . . dark. I wrote this down. *Nothing happened and yet the nothingness itself was an event. I wonder if that was the nothingness God experienced before He decided to create Earth and call it good.*' I think that sums it up." Celeste turned the page. "On the fourth night, I dreamed about my mother."

I was in my childhood bedroom. The room was just as I remembered it. Devoid of personality. Mother had taken away all my toys, my books, my posters, the letters left behind from my dad, who'd left town when I was very young and died after sending me three postcards and three handwritten letters. I was too young to read them myself, and Mother didn't want to read them for me. Then, when I started to learn to read, she snuck into my room, took the letters and cards, and then burned them. She showed me the ashes when I came back from school, just so I was sure they were gone for good. My mother never told me what my father died of, only that he was dead and we'd inherited a small amount of money from him, which was promised to me before she decided to take that too. In my bedroom, I never felt relaxed, I never felt safe, I always felt like I was being watched. There was no lock on the doorknob, so my mother could burst in whenever she liked, and she'd do so often in the middle of the night, howling as if she'd caught me committing a crime when all I was trying to do was sleep. I would go to school tired and come back home exhausted, and still, I was never allowed a proper night's sleep. It is what led to me struggling with insomnia throughout college (which got so bad I once "woke up" outside my dorm, laying down on a bench outside in my pajamas, surrounded by friends who'd been trying to wake me for twenty minutes and were close to calling an ambulance). Finding myself again in this bedroom, which held such horrible memories for me, I began to cry. I wanted to quiet myself, knowing even in my dream state that any noise I made would bring my mother charging into the room. I heard her footsteps in the hallway, hurrying like she'd just been waiting for me to make a mistake and was thrilled I finally had. I think that woman was only happy when I was in pain, and it was all she ever had to look forward to. As an adult, part of me wants to feel sad for her. She was angry and unhappy, and she never wanted a kid to begin with, much less a child as complicated as I was. And raising me wasn't easy. My father left shortly after I was born to be with a man. I wish he'd taken me, but I think even if he tried, she wouldn't have let him. She saw my own queerness as a stain left over from my father, a man she despised. So when I started to become myself, which happened early in my adolescence, she wanted to stamp it out. It is her hatefulness I remember most, which keeps me from being sympathetic to her own plight. I understand her dejection, her exhaustion, even her anger. I don't understand why she punished me for it when all I wanted to be was myself. Listening to her footsteps, the adult me and the child me existed at once inside my head. The child screamed internally, knowing a mistake had been made, that tonight would be a "bad" night. The adult me was thankful, because seeing the memory played out exactly as it felt validated all the hard thoughts I'd ever had about the woman who'd raised me. She opened the door and came into the room like a storm, yelling without pause, as if she didn't need to breathe the way us mere mortals did. Her tirades were always nonsensical, always about how I was damaging my own soul and that she'd rather die before I infected hers. She always brought in the shaving strop. It had once belonged to my father, and it was the only piece of him left behind in her house. The rest had been burned. It stung badly when she hit me with it, and there was never any question that she wouldn't. After yelling, I was always put over her legs and beaten. Bad enough that even sitting at school brought tears to my eyes. When teachers asked why I was crying, I had excuses, but the cause was consistent. It was because my mother beat me. Eventually, I learned not to cry . . . but I never learned a way to numb myself against the beatings. They always hurt the same, no matter how many I took. I just became better at hiding it. The dream version of my mother was too realistic. It was like she had found me as an adult and was forcing me to roleplay my own childhood with her, as if to make up for all the lost time since I ran away from home. She came toward my bed, lording over me, holding the leather strop (the one my father used to hone the edge of his shaving razor) over her head before bringing it down. The crack of the leather hitting my skin felt real . . . and I thought it would wake me up. But it didn't—

"Do I have to read the rest of it?" Celeste asked.

"Jesus. No, not if you don't want to. My God," Theo said.

"Sorry."

"No. Please don't apologize. Celeste . . . I'm so sorry." He reached over and took the journal out of her hands. For a terrifying moment, she thought he was going to read the rest of it himself, but he shut the book, set it on the coffee table, and gave Celeste his complete attention. He held her hands tightly and softly at the same time. "All I knew was you and your mother were estranged. I mean . . . you told me you'd fill me in on the whole story someday and I trusted you would but . . . I'm so sorry. I didn't mean to bring all of this up. Especially if you weren't ready to discuss it."

She'd known this was coming. Ever since her fourth dream, she'd started to embrace the exposure of her past. If it hadn't been for the nightmare, she didn't know when she'd have talked about it. Even with all Theo had shared with her, there never seemed to be an organic or natural moment for it. On the rare occasions when she'd come close, the words froze before they left her throat. One thing Celeste had always been good at was keeping her mother's secrets. Even now, far away from her influence, she still held what had been done to her as close to her chest as she could. Even to the people who loved and cared for her. None of her friends knew about the particulars of what had happened between Celeste and her mother, even if they knew it was bad. Even when she'd gone through a heavy drinking phase in college, she'd never once spilled the beans.

The only other person she'd told (aside now from Theo) was a complete stranger. It had happened randomly while riding the Trax home from a late-night shift when she'd been making ends meet at a bar that was designed to feel like an old-fashioned speakeasy. A large man with a bald head and a thick beard was sitting near her. When they were coming up to her stop, the bearded man started to slouch down, barely holding himself awake.

Without prompt, she'd caught his eyes just as they

were about to shut and said, "My mother beat me every night until I couldn't take it anymore and I ran away from home. My uncle legally adopted me and got me into a good school. If it wasn't for him, I'd be homeless now." She was so surprised she'd said it, she had to fight the urge to stop her hand from covering her mouth, as if she could somehow take back the words she'd let slip out of it. Her knees became tingly, and her stomach did a headstand. She worried she might vomit.

The sleepy bearded man opened his eyes and studied hers. After a moment of painful silence, he said, "That was nice of your uncle."

Then he crossed his arms, leaned his head back, and began to snore. By then, they had come to Celeste's stop. She ran off the cart, holding back tears. She felt as if she was holding her breath all the way down the street, around the corner, and up to her third-floor apartment. When she closed the door behind her, she collapsed right on her floor and sobbed.

That had been the last time she'd said any of it aloud.

Until now . . .

"I wasn't raised by her," she told Theo. "When I was fourteen, my uncle, Lucas, adopted me. I only lived in his house for a few years before he gave me enough money for college."

"I'd like to meet him someday—"

"You can't; he died." She sounded more emotionless than she intended. "Just like his brother-in-law . . . too young. He slipped in the shower and hit his head. The last time I saw my mother was at his funeral. She drove by a few times, and I think she didn't realize we all knew her car. Some people wanted her to come in. I didn't. I was glad she was scared to face me."

Celeste realized she was panting. Telling these stories was like swallowing thumbtacks. She caught her breath, refocused her gaze, and swallowed her tears.

"It made me feel powerful for the first time in my life," she said. "Just knowing that she was scared to see me in person. That for once, I was keeping her up at night. I slept like a baby that week. It didn't last, but it was nice for a while."

"I hadn't realized how much you'd gone through."

She tried to shrug.

"Seriously. Thank you for sharing—"

She didn't want to be complimented for having trauma, so she opened her journal again and summarized the next few nights of restless and weird dreams.

"On the fifth night, I dreamed about the nothingness again. It was really comforting. On the sixth night, I dreamed the nothingness broke, and I was underwater. I've dreamed about being underwater before, but usually, I'm panicked or drowning. In this dream, I could breathe the water, like I'd become amphibious. And last night . . ."

"What happened?" Theo asked when he couldn't

wait any longer.

"Last night . . . I dreamed about us going to the cabin. The details were already fuzzy when I woke up, but it felt kind of like . . . a transition was taking place." She closed her book. "There. And if you're wondering, yeah . . . I think the ritual may work. These dreams convinced me."

"You don't have to—"

"I do. I'll say it because I mean it. I was going to do all this at first just because I care about you, but now . . . I'm doing it for me too. So let's not waste any more time. Let's get started."

Now, it was Theo's turn to pause. "Are you sure?" he asked, his voice muted by the howling of the wind, the falling of new snow, the rustling of the trees closing in on them like titanic hands with unclean fingers.

"Yes," Celeste said. "I'm sure."

CHAPTER THREE

He opened his black doctor's bag again. He narrated for her, telling her what the items were as they were revealed, even though she'd been told about them before, when the ritual had initially been proposed. She figured he wasn't underestimating her memory, that he wanted to stress the importance of each item, and this, too, was somehow a part of what they were going to do this weekend.

Not only this weekend but tonight. It begins tonight. Right now. The preamble is over. We're in the thick of it now.

"These black candles will illuminate us," Theo said, revealing six of them, tied together with fuzzy twine. With his other hand, he took out their holders, which were greased with long-dried wax from previous rites.

On the coffee table, he organized the holders into a neat circle. One by one, he worked each candle from the bundle and stuck them in, keeping all but one upright. The crooked candle caught Celeste's eye. Before she could say anything, Theo was explaining its purpose.

"We only allow in what we want in. We will be vigilant tonight and tomorrow, but we're inviting a dark force into this place. This is an open doorway." He tapped the candle's wick with a nervous finger. "They will come in through here while the rest stand guard. Would you like to light them?"

She nodded.

He took a matchbox out of the bag. "Use a new match for each wick. Don't use any of the candles to light the others. I'll get the lights." He stood and went to shut off the kitchen and then the living room lights.

When he sat down, Celeste had saved the crooked candle for last. She handed back his matchbox, which went into the bag and was replaced with a new item.

"This is the only known artifact that remains of Ib, a kingdom some scholars debate even existed. They had no Bible, no records, no philosophers. They were prehistoric men who worshiped a strange god. It is this god who provides us our dreams, in the hopes it will once more be worshipped."

A chill ran down Celeste's spine. Everything Theo was saying sounded rehearsed. It was like he was putting on a one-man play for himself, and she just so happened to be voyeuristically watching.

"Hold it. Feel it. Memorize it."

She picked up the item. It was a chunk of stone with a symbol engraved on its surface, like a fossilized fish bought from a hokey gift shop. The symbol had ridges like bones. It was circular, with a jagged line cut through its middle. Several tendrils grew out of the circle like roots around the base of a tree.

"What is it?" Celeste asked.

"It's a sign," Theo stated much too bluntly. "No one knows what it was supposed to mean, but the theory is that it was a bad omen. That the city was sunk shortly after it was put up."

"It's so small. If it was meant to be a warning, it's not a very good one." She tried not to smile when Theo chuckled.

He turned serious again. The next to last item was revealed. A chunky goblet encrusted in plastic jewels. It looked like a craft made at a Christian summer camp.

He set it in the middle of the candle-lit circle.

"This is the cup," was all he said before dragging out the last item. "This is the knife."

He didn't even hesitate, which disturbed Celeste more than if he'd dragged the process out. Cleanly and swiftly, he gripped the curvy blade with one hand and the handle with the other. He pulled both apart, dragging a gash into his palm. Blood dribbled between his clenched fingers, and he seethed as he let it spill into the goblet.

"D-do I have to do that?" Celeste asked.

"You have to give something. It doesn't have to be blood."

She blushed.

"Even spit is enough."

A fine compromise, she thought lightly.

He set the knife back into the bag and searched around for the roll of gauze and tape he kept there. They were the only items in the black bag that one would actually expect to find on a doctor's person.

While Theo wrapped his hand, Celeste shifted her red hair away from her face, leaned over the candles, and worked up as much spit as she could. It fell out from her pursed lips in strands, merging with the coal-dark blood inside the cup. The white of her saliva was quickly tainted a wine-like crimson.

Thankful she wasn't being asked for any other fluids, she looked away from the circle and toward her partner. "Does it hurt?"

"A bit. Not bad. It's not super deep, but that's more blood than I've given the last few times." He suppressed a dry laugh. "I really want it to work for you, so I figured I'd go all in."

"I'd say that's sweet, but it's pretty gross."

He barked. "Here, want to look at it?" He started to pull the gauze he'd wound around his hand back, showing off the wound, which had gone from a gentle flow to a slight trickle. It really didn't look as bad as expected, but it was still alarming.

"We'll clean that, right?"

"Yes. Once we're done for the night," he said. "C'mon, we're almost there."

"Okay. Okay. What now?" She felt like she was playing with a Ouija board at a sleepover.

"Now, you close your eyes . . . and you think of Bokrug."

"Of what?"

Theo closed his eyes. "You don't have to know what it is. Only that it is."

"I don't under—"

"Just let whatever comes to mind come to mind. Focus on the name itself. Let it be all you think about. Bokrug . . . Bokrug . . . Bokrug." His voice trailed away as if he was driving off without her. For the last time, he said the name in a whisper, and then he was contemplatively quiet.

More than a bit confused, she closed her eyes and tried to think of how someone would even spell "Bokrug." Was it exactly as it sounded, or was she missing a silent letter, a hidden accent, something to the name that made it more complex than it already was? The name swirled through her head. Outside, the wind picked up. Inside, the candles flickered. And in Celeste's head, she thought, *Bokrug . . . Bokrug . . . Bokrug . . .*

Theo clapped his hands, surprising her. She looked over and saw he was leaning back, tilting his head as if his neck was broken. His lips parted, and a soft whistle of breath escaped him.

This isn't what I expected. I thought there'd be chanting, or dancing, or something like they show in the movies. This all feels so . . . simple, Celeste thought.

"Bokrug . . ." Theo said, his voice so low she could barely hear it. "There are still people in Ib . . ."

He sat upright, popped his eyes open, and shot a white-toothed smile at Celeste. "Okay, that's it!"

"That's it?" she asked.

"That's it!" He leaned forward and blew out the candles like it was his birthday.

The cabin was plunged into darkness.

It only lasted a few seconds before the lights flicked back on, and Theo came grinning back into the living room, picking at his bandage. But in those seconds, Celeste could have screamed. She'd felt hollow, as if her organs had all been vaporized, and the darkness had been so cloying not even sound could penetrate it. The harsh and wall-battering howl of the wind had ceased, and so, too, had the arrogant groans of the trees. It'd felt not like the nothingness from her dreams but more like the nothingness her mother had described when she told Celeste she'd be going to Hell when she died.

That's what Hell is. Not a lake of fire . . . but the absence of God.

"Are you okay?" Theo asked, sitting down on the sofa's edge, closer to Celeste. "You look a little freaked."

She shook her head and looked at the candles, watching the thin, almost watery lines of smoke rise from their smoldering wicks. And the goblet in the middle, with its deposit of blood and spit. She took them in, hardly believing such cheap items had caused her such distress but knowing what she and Theo had done had briefly done something magnanimous to her soul. Something that could not be ignored.

It had cut her off from God.

She didn't know how to put these thoughts into words, so instead, she shuddered.

"Hey, you okay?" Theo stood, came over, and knelt by her. He took her hands in his, not realizing he had bled through the gauze and his touch was wet.

She tried blinking away her concerns. "Yeah, I'm fine. Just got shook up for a moment. Maybe it's just the wind, but I just felt . . ." How could she explain it? She couldn't. "I just felt a bit spooked."

"You don't have anything to worry about," he said.

"Do I? What are we going to dream about tonight?"

"I can't tell you. But it isn't bad. It won't be . . . like the dream you had about . . ."

"My mom?" she asked.

He nodded. "It happens to me sometimes too. I'll dream about Lavinia, or about having a breakdown in front of a group of faceless students . . . but it doesn't happen often, and it never happens when the ritual is being actively performed. The Dream Cycle has more impressive things to show us than just . . . rehashing our own pasts."

"I still don't understand a lot of it. What's Bokrug?"

He shook his head. "That would spoil the surprise. Hey, are you going to be all right?"

She pulled in a breath. "Yeah. I was just rattled."

"If you want to stop, we can. You might still have some weird dreams but . . . nothing heavy—"

"No. I still want to do it. It's just . . . you know. It's weird."

"It is, yeah." He winced. "I hate to ask for a favor, but . . ."

"Yes. Go into the bathroom and wash it off. Do you guys have any first aid kits?"

"Dad keeps one in the closet upstairs. It probably should be under the sink, but he didn't like me and Rich playing with his stuff. Old habits and all."

"I'll get it."

"See you in a moment?"

"See you soon." She kissed him quickly before they parted.

When she came back downstairs, she stayed a moment in the living room, looking upon the goblet. Somehow, it had been emptied and cleaned . . . but she hadn't heard the kitchen sink running, and she'd only been gone for a minute or two at most.

Maybe something drank it, she thought.

Then she realized her eyes were making mistakes. The goblet was still dirty with human fluids.

No, I really looked at it. And the lights are on. I've never had trouble with my eyesight before—

It probably wasn't best to dwell on it for long.

What she needed to do was get to the bathroom, preferably before Theo bled out.

His hand was an easy fix. The wound wasn't a pretty sight, but Celeste was thankful when the blood flow slowed again without much of a fuss. It would probably be sealed and gone within a week, she assured him.

"Do you really cut yourself this deeply every time?" she asked.

"Just about," he replied. "Once, I went too far in, and I thought I'd have to drive myself to a hospital."

"*Ooph*. Don't tell me that!" she said as she worried over his wound.

Celeste cleaned it, doused it in peroxide, then bandaged it with an adhesive. Afterwards, she kissed it to make it "all better."

While she used the toilet, Theo leaned against the sink and studied his left hand, visibly struggling to stop himself from picking at the cleaned-up wound.

"It won't heal if you mess with it," she said.

"I never liked band-aids. It's hard for me to think about anything else when I have one on."

"What do you do when I'm not around? Just let it bleed?"

He shook his head. "My dad was a big 'walk it off' guy. If you couldn't walk it off, then it was a big deal. I'd just wrap it up for the night and air it out in the morning, and it'd be fine."

"How often have you done this?" she asked as she stood, pulling her pants back up. She was still a bit surprised by how comfortable she was with his presence during moments like this one. It was good Theo never leered at her the way previous boys had, their eyes and mouths constantly and overwhelmingly hungry.

"Once a year."

"Do you take all your girlfriends up here to tend to your wounds?"

"You're the first. I mean, my first girlfriend to do this with me. I've done it with . . . other occultists."

"Really?" She walked over to the sink, pushed him aside playfully with a hip-nudge, and washed her hands.

"I used to be online a lot. Ran into some people who shared my interests. A few of us met and did it— oh, how long ago was that? Four years ago? No. It was five years ago. Good people. Shane, Lucas, and Wrath. Afterwards, we all kind of went our own ways, but they were really into it. Took it seriously and had some amazing dreams. Before then, I tried with an old friend from high school. He's a writer too. Much better than me. Writes dramas. Anyways, he just wanted an excuse to go to a cabin and get drunk. I think he was really upset when he saw I was serious about all the 'voodoo.' He said it was horseshit. I tried convincing him otherwise. I think I scared him off because we never really saw each other in person again. I still feel pretty bad about it."

"Sorry," she said, unsure what else to offer. Celeste turned off the hot water and sat on the counter, swinging her legs like she was dipping them in a swimming pool. "So, if I wasn't open to it . . . it wouldn't even work?"

"If you weren't open to it, you wouldn't have had any dreams before coming out here." He crossed his arms. "Hey, do you want to try something else tonight?"

"Something fun?" She gave him her best bedroom eyes. A perfect combination of flickering lashes and blushed cheeks.

"Well, that too . . . but I was thinking—sometimes drugs make it stronger."

"You mean I'll hallucinate tonight and call it a dream tomorrow?" She was a little disappointed.

"No. Just, like, weed. Nothing crazy. I don't come out here to drop acid."

"We haven't ever smoked together before. I honestly didn't know you . . . imbibed."

"I don't like to do it often. Just when the Dream Cycle is about to kick in. It makes me feel more perceptive. Like, I can focus better on the finer details in the dreams."

"I'm down. Did you bring anything? I sort of expected to be sober this weekend, so I hope you weren't relying on—"

"I have some stowed away." He put his finger to his lips. "Don't tell my mom. It'd break her heart."

"My lips are sealed. But while we're disappointing your mom, how about a shower?"

"I'd like that," he replied.

She stepped in front of him, put her arms over his shoulders, and fell against him. As they kissed, one of his hands crept down toward her backside. She could feel him hardening against her. She touched him through his pants, feeling the weight of his sex in the palm of her hand. It was warm like the last embers of a fire.

Theo leaned into her, letting his body and hers act on their own impulses. He squeezed her rump with both hands, then brought one up to stroke her throat, touching her chin with his thumb quickly.

"I love the way you taste," he said when their lips parted.

"Then taste me," she breathed, speaking so low that even if they weren't alone, no one would have heard her but him. Their intimacy was their secret, not because they were ashamed of it but because neither of them felt like anyone else had a right to it.

He knelt down before her, lifting the hem of her shirt so he could spread kisses up her belly and then back down toward the jutting edge of her hip. Then he worked her pants off, leaving them buttoned and tugging them. Slowly, he drew them down the lengths of her legs, following their trail with his lips, his tongue, and with small nibbles. When she stepped away from her pants, he was already moving her blue panties aside so her could kiss her between her flexing thighs.

He filled his mouth with her. She slipped in, lavished by his tongue and even the sharp edges of his teeth. His mouth was like a wet furnace. She curtailed her desire to pump her hips, to make herself cum before they'd even gotten started.

Celeste's hands ran through his hair, down toward the back of his skull, holding him into her pelvis so she was all he could smell, and taste, and see.

"Careful," she said, more to herself than to her lover. She let him suck her for a few seconds more, and then he continued the ritual (that word had such a different meaning now, it felt improper in this context) of pulling her clothes off of her body.

He hauled her shirt up, stopping just when her breasts were uncovered. He beheld them with marvel, as if he'd never seen them before. Sometimes, she stared at them with the same sense of wonder, standing in front of her bedroom mirror and holding them as if they'd sprung onto her chest while she was sleeping.

While he massaged her, teasing her nipples until they were full, she undid his pants, lowering his zipper as though frightened his penis would leap out at her. It was already erect, protruding between her hands, pulsating with excitement.

"In the shower," Celeste said, speaking directly into his mouth. "Please."

After they'd made love, each as slick as pudding, their mouths weary with kisses and yet unable to stop, their bodies shattered, their fluids swirling down the drain between their feet, Celeste had almost forgotten all about magic rituals, Bokrug, and the Dream Cycle.

They took turns drying each other off. The process of dressing into their nightclothes was just as much an erotic act as undressing had been, both helping each other, exploring their shared bodies with curious, wandering hands and gentle mouths.

Celeste was cozy and happy in her silk pajamas, and Theo wore a pair of old, loosened pajama bottoms. They hung precariously off his hips, which Celeste didn't dare poke fun at. She liked how he looked in them too much to encourage him to buy a pair with a tighter elastic waistband.

Before coming upstairs and redressing, he'd dashed into the bedroom near the front door. He showed her he kept his weed stash hidden under a loose floorboard.

"When'd you find that?" she asked as he took out a tin candy box and opened it so she could see a sealed Ziploc bag filled with green.

"Back when I was a kid. I used to keep my army toys in there. It was their 'bunker.' Then, when I was a teenager, it's where I kept my nudie mags."

"If your mother only knew."

"I'm joking. I kept my pornos in the tree house. They probably got blown into the creek a long time ago. Or they got rained on until they turned to mulch. Or Dad found them. Either way, they aren't there anymore. Not that I need 'em nowadays." He winked.

"Great. You really know how to make a girl feel special." She pouted.

He responded by kissing her cheek, then getting up

and dashing naked out of the room, bringing the box with him.

Now, they sat across from each other in bed, the tin box between them. She watched as her man tried to roll a joint, but he had butterfingers.

"I can usually do this," he said as a stream of grass fell out of one end of the joint.

"Give it." She held out her hand, palm open.

"I'm going to blame my injury," he said.

"Phooey. I could do this with one hand. Watch." She put her left hand behind her back and tried to roll a joint with the right. All she did was mash the paper. When it was over, the joint looked like a garbage bag, split at the seams. "Okay . . . it's a little harder than the movies made it seem."

Theo laughed, his eyes alight. "It was a good effort."

"I'll make a real one," she assured him, going back to square one and using both hands. In the end, they had an adequate cigarette, which Celeste sparked happily. After two long tokes, she passed it to her partner, who inhaled and coughed.

"You sure you've done this before?" she joked.

"I always cough. Everyone tells me I'll get over it, but . . . the first one is always the worst." He pulled in and held it, then let out a smooth stream of grey smoke. He tried to keep his composure . . . but another volley of coughs surged through him. It was enough to make him teary-eyed but not enough to make Celeste feel bad for laughing.

"You need some water?"

"Yes, please."

When she came back, she had two glasses of water and a bottle of vodka by the neck.

"We're drinking too?"

"I am. Not much, don't worry."

"Well, I am worried. Alcohol doesn't mix well with dreams."

"It doesn't?" She frowned. "Weed is fine . . . but not booze?"

"It may sound arbitrary, but I've done this enough to know what works and what doesn't."

Celeste moaned. "But your parents have such good taste!" She held the bottle out for him to take. He grabbed it, looked it over, then politely set it aside. "Fine," Celeste relented before slipping back into bed.

She lay on her back, and he came toward her. He fit the joint between her lips, and she inhaled. When she was done holding it in her lungs, she put her hands on his cheeks and blew into his open mouth. He didn't cough this time.

"Hey," he said, his voice husky with smoke.

"Hey yourself." She blinked wearily.

"Are you okay? With all of this?"

"Of course." She put her arms around him, interlocking her fingers behind his head, letting the joint simmer in her mouth.

"I love you." Barely a whisper.

"I love you too." Spoken out of the side of her mouth, around the cigarette.

They readjusted, snuggling under the covers. Taking turns with the joint before it was finished, Celeste and Theo talked in soft voices, as if there were ears in the next room even though they'd never been this isolated before. It was, she realized with some trepidation, as if they were on a covert honeymoon. She half hoped he'd pop the question before the week was over.

I'd say yes. I really would, Celeste thought as she dropped the butt into her water glass on the nightstand. They curled up close . . . and fell asleep in each other's arms.

C H A P T E R   F O U R

She was standing just beyond the sliding glass doors, her feet chilled by the snow. She wanted to wrap her arms around herself to warm up, but she couldn't move. Instead, she looked forward . . . beyond the hills surrounding the cabin . . . beyond the creek that ran like a varicose vein through the white snow . . .

I'm dreaming and I know it. What's that called?

Lucid dreaming.

She'd read that if you looked at your hands during a dream, you would then have some power over your dreaming self. You could (sometimes) control what direction you walked, what you said, or even the environment around you. She tried it now, but it proved nearly impossible. She was locked in place, trapped in the cold and in her own body. Theo had told her to just let the dreams happen, so she resigned herself to it, allowing her feet to lead the way. Inside, she tried to relax, to take in what she was seeing and feeling.

Enjoy the ride, she told herself. *Or . . . try to.*

She took an involuntary step forward. The snow

was so cold it burned. She wished she could dream herself a pair of boots.

I'm in my pajamas. I feel just like I did before I went to sleep. Drowsy and comfy from the waist up. Only everything below my hips is in the Arctic!

She wished Theo could be with her. Even just a dream-version of him. He could keep her company and walk her through the process as it happened. Instead, she felt her all-too-real fear of the unknown crawl upon her.

Please put me somewhere warm, she hoped as she took another jaunty step into the blasting winter winds. It was dark out. The trees were so bare they looked like glowing lampposts. Their limbs stretched toward her, each ending in either a gnarled, geriatric hand or a gleaming arrow tip. The roots looked like a tangled net of mesh and veiny tissue peering out from the piled snow with wet, dark eyes.

Everything around her was distorted and jagged. Like a walleye lens had been put over the environment. The ground itself seemed to bend and shift to the whims of the filter. The road became rocky and strange as Celeste walked it, as even her dream-feet struggled to know when the ground would rise and when it would fall. There was nothing easy, in this dream, about the simple act of walking. She recalled, distantly, her eighth grade health class. The kids had been made to wear vision-distorting goggles and were challenged to shoot a basket in the gymnasium while under a sort of simulated influence. She hadn't made the shot, but she'd tried her best, hoping to prove her teacher wrong when he said it was impossible, simply because she hadn't liked him.

If her feet weren't freezing, she would have enjoyed the memory. Instead, she clanged back to the present, to "reality," to the dream. She was headed toward the tree line now, where it looked like the ground had inverted, turning into something like a volcanic bowl rather than a rising mountain. The bowl shrank, becoming a smoking meteor crater, and then it expanded again, like wet clay in inexperienced hands. Then it was flat and wide, and there was no snow left beyond the line of stiff trees.

If she'd had her faculties with her, Celeste would have sprinted toward the dry patch, just to give her feet a break. The cold felt like it was sliding underneath the flesh of her heels. It twanged her nerves and burrowed into the cores of her legs.

It's what I've always thought frost bite would feel like. Maybe I was right and this is accurate. Or maybe the dream is catering to my beliefs.

Either way, this one felt much more realistic than any of the previous ones had. Those dreams were realistic but blurry. This felt like life itself was being morphed into a dream, as if her nightmares had escaped her head and were now forcing her surroundings to comply to their whims. One was certainly scarier than the other.

Her feet carried her, dragging through the crystalline mounds. She wondered if the cold was drawing the blood out of her, if she was leaving red footprints in her wake. Through the trees she went and down a small slope, and then the ground was flat and craggy. Rocks bit into her already injured feet, making her flinch and whine.

Theo had said nothing about pain. He'd promised her weird visions of otherworldly places, not frostbite and shark-toothed stones. When she woke up, she was going to scream at him, or run into the bathroom, lock the door, and cry. Or perhaps she'd just be too thankful to be awake to do anything at all but lie on her back and gasp for breath.

Did something go wrong? Have I made some kind of mistake? If so, Theo didn't notice. Maybe I should have bled into the goblet. Maybe chickening out gets you punished. If this happened to him, if he'd endured pain like this, wouldn't he have told me it was a possibility? That this ritual isn't completely harmless?

Unless he had known and was doing this to her intentionally.

She couldn't grapple with it. Theo was nothing but caring and considerate. If he knew she could be hurt, he would have warned her. Certainly, she didn't know everything about him, but she knew enough. There was nothing sadistic, spiteful, or cruel about Theo.

Wonder if anyone ever thought that before going home with Dahmer.

She couldn't afford to think that way. It wasn't helpful, and all it did was add to her discomfort. The snow and the rocks had shorn the skin off her feet, and now the sand and salt was burning her from the inside out.

A stone with a pointed tip speared her foot. She

wanted to lift it faster, but the leg lingered as if it was relishing the pain, twisting onto the ground before finally taking its next harrowing step. A soggy red footprint was left behind her.

She wanted to scream. Nothing would come out. She couldn't even force her mouth open.

Celeste realized she hadn't blinked. The air around her was thick and wet, making her already teary vision turn blurry. She couldn't see where she was going, only that it was dark ahead. SO dark, she knew she'd be blind. And what then? Would she walk sightless into the void? Off of a cliff? She hoped for a cliff. At least that would put a stop to whatever this was.

The wind was behind her, ruffling her hair the way her uncle did when she was being precocious, like she was still a little kid. But everything else reminded her of her mother. Of the smacks of the leather strop, of the hard words which put ice picks in her heart, of the burning water and the wire scrub, of the way she made Celeste stand in the corner until her legs felt like the smoldered remains left behind by a roaring forest fire (sometimes for hours, sometimes for an entire night before school).

This is how I felt back then. So exhausted and brutalized. So pained, with no other choice but to walk through it. If this is the embodiment of a metaphor, some sort of visual therapy, then I don't need it.

I want to wake up.

The rocks gave way to fresh snow. The icy cold seeped into her fresh wounds, chilling her from the inside. She'd reached the end of the flattened ground that had once been a crater. Now, she was trudging again through bare-treed woods. All around her, she could hear the wind whistle, and she could hear boughs bending and creaking like old rocking chairs.

The desire to awaken fought the desire to know more, to clear her eyes and see where she was and where she was headed. She was relieved when the force controlling her saw fit to restore her ability to blink. It came back jarringly, and she was addicted to the sweet simplicity of blinking. Intentionally, she closed and opened her eyes, clearing the tears and working through the strain. Some of her blood vessels had burst, staining the whites of her eyes red. If she'd been denied the ability to blink for much longer, she imagined her eyes swelling and popping like over-inflated balloons.

Then, to her surprise, she looked down and saw her hands. They were held ahead of her, zombielike. The moment she saw them, she twiddled her fingers all on her own. The knuckles popped like firecrackers, resonating through the woods in spite of the battering wind.

Something rose up her throat. Fast like running water, it burst out of her mouth.

"Oh . . ."

Just a single word, and was she ever grateful for it! Pantingly, she slowed her feet and wavered in place, languishing in the joy of *feeling* . . . in the reclamation of her body.

But she was aware these were now privileges rather than rights. Whatever had forced her out of the cabin and into the woods could easily take back its power. Whatever it wanted, she'd do. She wasn't in control; she had just been given a looser leash. Still, she flexed her hands, blinked her eyes, and worked her mouth.

She turned around and was horrified to see ribbons of blood led from her feet to the distant cabin in a jagged puzzle-piece path. The cold had frozen the blood, making it look as bright red as paint against the snow and inky dark on the rocks. The blood bisected the flat, rocky spot that had grown out of the darkness.

The left half began to shift. It happened soundlessly, as if a tectonic shift was nothing more than a breath. The left side of the circle dipped down, making the right appear elevated. The two halves were still divided by Celeste's blood, but a new fluid rose up from between the stones, seeping in to fill their gaps. It was as if a giant hand was squeezing a dishtowel from underneath the surface of the earth and the water was impossibly falling *up* rather than down.

Celeste neared the circle, her eyes narrow and her breath still. She didn't want to make a sound for fear that whatever was happening would take new notice of her. Respectfully and patiently, she watched as the left side of the circle became a pond, and then a lake—and then an ocean.

—an *ocean* . . .

She'd been transported. It happened so fast it put a fist in her throat. She stumbled as if she'd been pushed from behind, and leaned against a tree to keep her balance. Pressing one side of her face into the bark, she tried her best to take in what she was seeing before she was too overwhelmed to concentrate.

She was still in the forest, still surrounded by winter's snow, still crowded by leafless trees with knotted roots and skeletal limbs . . . but she was looking through an invisible wall and into another place. A small, moonlit cove, where the wind pushed waves up from the salty sea and toward the stones.

She inhaled, tasting the all-too-familiar tang of the ocean, of brine, of dead fish. It was so real she'd almost forgotten she was dreaming, still in bed beside Theo. And she was still hurting too.

Please don't make me walk into the sea, she prayed, already imagining how the water would sting her frost- and stone-tattered feet.

There was no longer a cabin. Just a wall of stone, which rose up into the night higher than a skyscraper. The wall was honeycombed with caves, and each cave was illuminated by strobing firelight. The orange glow combatted with the pale moonlight, turning into something green and sickly. She saw elaborate ladders stretch up from the shore toward the caves, constructed not from wood but from a substance that looked like ivory and coral. It was twisted and intricate, with steps that looked like dragons wrapped around the ladder's legs, meeting in the middle, where they swallowed their own scaly tails.

Figures stood at the mouths of the caves. They were hard to distinguish, but there was *something* inhuman about them. They had arms and legs, but their backs were humped and their heads looked—*sharp.*

Almost as if each one was adorned with an arrowhead-ed helmet.

They swayed and wavered, precariously close to the edges of their caves where their ladders stopped or diverted.

They were chanting.

Celeste stepped behind the tree, bracing like she expected gravity to fail her. In quiet terror, she listened to the voices. They streamed down from the caves, amplified by them. Even the thunderous crash of an unhappy wave could not mute their coordinated, unified voice.

Many of the words were nonsense, but one stood out to her. One she'd heard Theo use before. This particular section of their mantra was repeated more often than the others. It punctuated every sentence, and it grew louder and more frenzied as they went.

"IÄ . . . IÄ . . . *Bokrug!*"

Bokrug.

Close your eyes . . . and think of Bokrug.

Theo had told her it did not matter what Bokrug was. He'd seemed delighted, even, when she'd asked, as if the whole point had been to deny her an explanation.

While she still did not know, she was starting to get an idea.

Bokrug was what these people worshipped. It was the name of an old god. One of Theo's "forgotten" gods. The sort that fell out of favor when new religions colonized previous ones. A god that probably had temples and artifacts once upon a time, but those were all buried. Swallowed by the sea or smashed when the caves collapsed. Maybe someone did find remnants of his worshipers, but there was no way to decipher what it was they believed in, especially when all that was left behind were fragments of fragments.

Bokrug.

A sea god, like Poseidon, Celeste theorized.

Hard waves dropped onto the fragile shore, thrown by the ancient deity's colossal hands. The god was fuming and tempestuous, calmed only when he was worshiped the right way. And even then, even when he was appeased, he'd be quick to anger at a moment's notice.

Bokrug.

She closed her eyes, and unlike before . . . a picture began to grow.

She imagined something swollen and green, with claws as long as her arms and eyes like cracked rubies, with a mouth that produced so much sea foam it looked like a white beard that trailed down his expanding chest. Each breath was a hurricane. Each stomp of his webbed foot shook the earth, causing rocks to fall out of the caves like marbles from the hands of impatient children, bouncing and breaking as they fell, then becoming a rainstorm of pebbles that could shoot through bodies like bullets.

Bokrug.

They chanted his name, growing more fervent as

the waves crawled up the cove, spraying the lower caves. She could hear people crying now, screeching in an incoherent language that may not have been a language at all. Maybe they were scared.

She was.

She was actually terrified.

Her heart thumped in her chest, beating to match the chant—

"IÄ! IÄ! Bokrug!"

It would have sounded silly, that name, in any other context. But here, facing the mass insanity claiming his people, the name Bokrug struck her like lightning. It burrowed into her chest, gripping whatever it could, and then it tore out in a flush of red panic. She wanted to run but knew doing so would only delay the inevitable. She'd come here to see, and see she would. Whether she wanted to or not.

The sea burbled and splashed. White arms smashed into the stones, punching new holes into the walls. If Bokrug wanted, he could put a wave *over* the cliff, flooding the caves and washing out their occupants. The ladders could so easily be broken if Bokrug so desired. They'd snap like rotten timber, and the people would be trapped, forced to starve to death unless they were brave enough to leap into the sea and face Bokrug's wrath personally.

It was no wonder, Celeste realized, this god had been forgotten. He was not loving, nor was he kind. He was a looming foot willing and able to squash the ants below him, hesitating only because they'd found a way to amuse him.

The sea split down the middle, similar to the way the stony circle had fractured after she'd walked across it. A long, dark line grew from the shore and extended into the nothingness beyond. The darkness expanded, growing until it opened. A slit in the ocean that led into pure nothingness—a void similar to the one she'd found comfort in when she'd dreamed. It was an absence of being, of light, of everything but Bokrug.

The chanters had lost their unity. They screamed and garbled, each making their own proclamation. They constructed prayers in desperation, pushing their individual voices so they may be spared in case Bokrug wanted their neighbors.

They teetered on the edges of their cliffs. One narrowly avoided falling when a rock broke away beneath him. He stumbled back, startled, and then crumpled to his knees and bowed low, covering his head in his hands and shouting pleas for mercy. Meanwhile, the rock smashed into the cliffside, broke apart, and spat dusty stones in multiple directions. One pebble slipped through the gap, disappearing into the void. It was as if it had been consumed by shadows.

And then the moonlight itself shifted, falling not on the shore but above it. Toward the top of the cliff and upon its edge. It was a spotlight now, filtered through steadily thickening and stormy clouds. Lightning shattered the sky, further brightening what Bokrug wanted to see.

Celeste was horrified.

A young maiden was standing on her tiptoes,

facing the void. She was beautiful, even with her sickly green skin. Her flaxen hair fell over her shoulders and obscured her breasts. She was clothed in an immodest ceremonial uniform, looking like a nymph dancing on an ancient urn. She'd covered her eyes with cloth, obscuring much of her face.

One voice rose above the noise of the ocean. It was from a cave close to the ground, and it carried far. Celeste could hear a man enunciate his words carefully, but she had no clue what he was saying. She could guess.

She supposed the man was a priest and he was offering a sacrifice.

When his voice froze, the woman cried out, not even letting a moment pass between his prayers and her own throaty proclamation. It was a sharp bleat that ended in a mournful wail. The sound that a coyote only seems capable of making from a great distance.

She held her arms up, revealing her hands were tied together with a golden material that looked too thick and glossy to be mere rope. Celeste guessed the material had been built around her hands, locking them together. The woman had had to walk all the way up the cliff without being able to separate her hands, and now she was going to die this way.

Celeste's heart beat rapidly again as the woman swayed in place, trying to work up the nerve to jump. She'd been a willing sacrifice, Celeste theorized, but it was always hard to jump when you had to. Even if you felt there was no other option.

In the shadows behind her blinking eyelids, she

saw a vision of herself when she was a child, walking home from school. There was a short bridge that led from the road to her neighborhood, and beneath it ran a shallow creek that was always chilly, even in the summertime. On her way home, she'd lean over the railing and drop stones into the water, watching them splash before sinking. Watching bubbles rise up even after the rocks were obscured. The water murky and grimy, like it came not from a spring but from a soiled swamp. It was designed to smother and drown.

The fall wasn't long, but sometimes, she thought if she went headfirst—

No . . . Celeste thought. *No, Theo . . . I don't want to see this. Why on Earth would you ever think I'd want to see something like this?*

The maiden leaned forward, which made Celeste's heart beat faster before it stopped. She felt like she'd been in a head-on collision and this was the microsecond before the head-punching deployment of an airbag.

Then the maiden fell. She didn't jump but rather *hopped* off the cliff's edge. The motion was almost dainty and polite, like a ballerina lifting up before a pirouette.

The fall was not quite so graceful.

Like Celeste's stones over the railing, the green-skinned woman dropped hard and fast. The wind lifted the stray strips of cloth hanging from her body, making it look as if she was a kite abandoned by the breeze. She swirled all the way down, spinning in the air until she was turned upside down. Her arms were held ahead of her as if she was attempting a suicidal dive. Her fingers were clasped into an unbreakable knot, while her legs kicked involuntarily. She was trying to swim through the air and toward the hole, like she wanted it over and done with and her kicks could get her there faster.

The crowd watched, their poorly lit faces falling with her. Whether this sacrifice was going as planned, Celeste couldn't tell. What she could see was mass sadness. They, like the maiden, knew this was something she had to do, but none had wanted it. No one took pleasure in seeing a beautiful girl die.

She fell into the sea-splitting chasm—and Celeste fell with her.

Celeste's soul had been roughly yanked from her body and was rocketed into the darkness. She floated behind the falling maiden, watching as the darkness seized her.

The green-skinned woman screamed once, but her open mouth filled with wet shadows before the sound could reach its highest pitch. Even the dignity of protest was stolen from her before it could be realized.

It's eating her, Celeste thought, trying to observe like a documentarian. But no matter how hard she tried, she couldn't separate herself from what she was seeing. It went beyond the horror of a nightmare because nightmares had never felt so real (nor so vicious). *The shadows themselves are eating her.*

Celeste had been denied the basic functions she'd had since birth. The ability to close her eyes was lost to her now that she had no eyes, now that she was seeing this happen the way God saw all things. Trapped in omnipotence.

Wake up . . . wake up . . . Please, God, why can't I wake up?

The darkness gnawed into the maiden, swaddling her before consuming her. And then there was nothing left.

It was the same as her dreams. She drifted in the absence, not drowning or compressed by it but simply permitted to *be* in it. Only this time, she knew the void had teeth. That every time she'd dreamed of it, she'd been putting herself in danger.

I just want to wake up . . .

There was something else in the darkness with her.

It was the consumer, and it had chosen a shape.

Ahead of her, it floated, suspended in the shadows like a cell in a blood stream. She watched as it neared, fearsome and titanic, larger than a warship and just as threatening.

Bokrug.

The water lizard.

The king.

The lord of Ib, the civilization that lived by the sea and were wise enough to fear it.

It came toward her, gliding through the darkness as easily as a tadpole, swishing its mighty tail back and forth and clawing the void with its sickle-shaped talons. The closer it got, the bigger it became. Celeste saw now that a battleship was a weak comparison.

A battleship would make an inadequate toothpick to this massive beast.

Its mouth dropped open, yawning wide. Its teeth were overgrown and pock-marked, looking less like fangs and more like fractured chunks of coral refashioned into arching walls. Each "tooth" was as tall as the Empire State Building. Some were taller.

Plumes of smokey residue rose from the vortex that was Bokrug's throat. Like smog from a smokestack, the substance wafted around, curling and corkscrewing before expanding and dissipating. Unlike smoke, this substance was a thick green color, darker than the green skin of the people from the caves—it reminded Celeste of patches of seaweed washed ashore after a storm.

In the foggy discharge, she saw screaming faces. They were voiceless, crying out for help that would never come. She knew, somehow, these faces belonged to his previous sacrifices. The maiden who'd been devoured was now one of thousands who suffered eternally within Bokrug, comforted only by the tenuous fact that their suffering meant their people still lived on the surface above them. That maybe, perhaps, Bokrug would be merciful to them. And if he wasn't, then at least they'd only drown.

This was worse.

Worse than death.

Worse than terror.

Worse than Hell.

And the silence was the worst part of all.

Bokrug did not roar or growl. He did not announce himself with thunder. Instead, he crept toward Celeste, becoming all she could see. He filled the darkness of the void in stealthy quietude, becoming bigger . . . and bigger . . . while his mouth became a void unto itself. Wider . . . and wider . . .

Celeste wanted to scream (futile as it may have been), and she discovered she couldn't.

All she could do was stare in awe as Bokrug's mouth slowly, almost placidly, closed around her.

She was cast into a deeper darkness than she had ever thought possible. The darkness she imagined when she wondered what it was like to be in a coma.

And then . . .

Part Two

The Outsider

"A certain atmosphere of breathless and unexplainable dread of outer, unknown forces must be present, and there must be a hint expressed with a seriousness and portentousness becoming its subject, of that most terrible conception of the human brain—a malign and particular suspension or defeat of those fixed laws of Nature which are our only safeguard against assaults of chaos and the daemons of unplumbed space."

H.P. Lovecraft, from his introduction to his essay "Supernatural Horror in Literature."

CHAPTER FIVE

. . . she was awake.

Consciousness hit her like cold water, drawing her upright with a deep, body-shaking gasp. Convulsively, she rolled over and vomited, throwing her dinner onto the floor beside the bed. Her mind was a flurry of panic. She struggled to grasp what was happening, what *had h*appened. In these seconds after waking, it was like her body was trying to reject her soul.

What was that? she thought as she expelled the last bits from her stomach. She rolled onto her back, breathing sharply, cringing at the mixture of foul tastes on her tongue. *That wasn't a dream. It really happened. I felt it all like I was there. And that . . . that thing in the ocean . . . it swallowed me!*

She wept at the memories. Unlike before, she doubted she'd have to rush to her journal to keep this dream from fading away. It was tattooed on her brain, just as vivid as her childhood trauma. When she closed her eyes, she was returned not to the darkness, not to the void, but to the *mouth*. That mouth was bigger than a city.

She saw also the plumes of green smog rising up from the beast, each cloud filled with muted faces stuck in agonized screams.

If I hadn't woken up, I'd be in there still. I'd be consumed, and then I'd live forever in the smoke—

She turned over, unsure how she was going to tell Theo about what she'd seen. It was so clearly not what he'd witnessed, because if he had . . . he never would have repeated this horrible ritual. Either way, she knew their cabin retreat had come to an end. She was going to insist they pack their things and go, and on the way down the mountain, she'd decide whether or not she ever wanted to see him again.

It depended on what he told her. Whether she believed him. All that mattered at the moment was getting home, getting away from this terrible place, and never seeing Theo's horrible black doctor's bag again.

The bed was empty.

She stuck her hand out and patted Theo's side as if he'd somehow sunk himself into the mattress and was hiding just beneath the sheets.

She wanted to call his name, but something made her pause.

Outside, the wind roared. It sounded like a set of floodgates had been opened.

She sat upright and looked around the dark bedroom.

It was empty.

Celeste flicked on the lamp on the nightstand. The

yellow light offered her only an orb of comfort, but it seemed to make the shadows creeping toward her much darker. It was like the light was being pushed back into the bulb by something invisible. The darkness itself—

Don't think that way. That's crazy talk.

Was it? Celeste didn't think so. After everything that had just happened to her, she was starting to think some of those primordial fears all children eventually grow out of were more valid and serious than they'd been treated. There could be something under the bed or hiding in the closet, and the darkness on its own was a sort of monster now. Amorphous and shadowy, with jagged edges that could cut through flesh—Where was Theo? She wished he'd go ahead and come up the steps, or cough, or even belch. She needed some indication she wasn't alone in this cabin, that he hadn't walked into the storm in his sleep and vanished.

He's probably in the bathroom. Just give it a moment and you'll hear the toilet flush. Or he got himself a midnight snack. Just be patient, Celeste. Don't fly off the handle, she thought to herself.

Quietly, Celeste drew her knees up to her chin and hugged herself. She felt chilly but didn't want to get out of bed to turn up the heat. She wanted Theo to come upstairs and reassure her. She wanted to go back to her own bed, where she was certain she'd sleep soundly.

Where was he?

She considered leaving the bed. Leaning over, she saw the pile of sick she'd left on her side. Some had spattered the blankets, which sent a new wave of revulsion through her. It felt like a cat was standing on her belly, kneading her with rough paws.

Celeste closed her eyes and straightened up.

Then she opened her eyes because closing them really didn't help. It just reminded her, once again, of the horrible place that had torn itself into the ocean.

It reminded her of the falling maiden who looked like a Martian from an old movie with her green skin and scanty clothes.

Maybe that's where the idea of space invaders came from. They're dreams from a lost society—left over like ghosts in an old house. Maybe they left us, and our notion of visiting UFOs is all screwed up. Maybe they weren't coming to say Hi or to help us build pyramids. They were just driving by to see what became of the planet they abandoned!

More crazy talk. Calm down, Celeste. It was her uncle's voice, rational and smooth. Celeste's uncle was everything her mother wasn't, and she recalled the way he spoke when she needed guidance. Sometimes, she felt like he could organize her thoughts better than she could, especially when she was in the middle of a breakdown.

Is that what this is?

Sure. You woke up vomiting from a nightmare that was so intensely realistic, it has you thinking aliens are real!

Well, Uncle Lucas, they might be. Although now, I'm thinking maybe they didn't come from Earth or space at all. I think they came from the ocean.

The name came to her like a bad smell. Bokrug, the water lizard. An old god, worshiped by an old people. And he'd been terrible. Unforgiving and stormy, what Celeste had seen of him was enough to convince her there was good reason this beast was no longer worshipped.

C'mon, Theo . . . where are you?

Finally mustering up the strength to speak, she called his name. It was a chirp of a sound, and she had to focus on her second attempt.

"Theo? Theo! I'm awake!"

No response came to her. All she could hear was the wailing of the wind. It caressed the house, battered the windows, and made sounds that brought monsters to mind. She gathered up the blankets and buried herself under them, peeking out from them and staring at the nearest window, which looked like the entrance to a mineshaft. Sometimes, she caught sight of snow flurries, but even those seemed dark and polluted. The snow left snotty smears on the surface of the glass.

"Theo?" she called.

He wasn't there.

He'd abandoned her.

She was all alone . . . all alone . . . all alone in the darkness . . .

Then she heard footsteps.

They came slowly up the creaky wooden steps.

She considered grabbing the lamp. If the door opened and a green-skinned monster came barreling into the room, she doubted smashing a lamp on its head would kill it, but it could give her time to escape.

Escape where?

If Theo had abandoned her, he'd taken the car. Their only way up and down the mountain. If she bolted outside, she'd freeze to death.

Maybe that was preferable. Easier, certainly, than being dissolved by shadows and turned into an ethereal green smog inside the mouth of an immense deity from another dimension.

The footsteps stopped at the top of the stairs. Celeste could hear a gentle pull of breath. It wasn't enough to go on, but she hoped it had sounded like Theo.

"Theo?" she asked.

He didn't respond.

The bedroom door swung open.

The wind stopped howling.

Celeste screamed when her mother stepped into the room. She had to bend over to fit through the door, as she'd grown four extra feet taller since Celeste had last seen her.

Her clothes had stayed the same size, meaning they barely fit her now that she was an incredible nine feet tall. The ends of her Christmas sweater's sleeves were just at her elbows, and the hem of her dress-skirt rustled below her knees. Her flesh was way too pale. It was as if Celeste's mother had spent the last decade hiding in a cave, allowing a black-hooded torturer to stretch her out on a medieval rack.

The woman's long, white hair fell around her head like a bridal gown. She wore a clownish smile, exposing a mouth full of horse teeth—thick, blocky, and yellowed.

Her eyes were also altered. They were milk white and rumpled, as if they'd been replaced with golf balls.

Celeste stood and backed away from the bed, steering herself toward the corner furthest from the uncanny woman that had once been her mother.

"Do you dream of me?"

The woman lifted her hands and started to walk toward Celeste in slow motion, as if she as running through water. Her words were whispered, but Celeste heard them nonetheless. It was like they'd been spoken directly into her ears from behind, like her mother was throwing her voice better than any ventriloquist.

"I dream of you. I dream of hurting you."

Celeste roared in panic, clutching at her chest with one hand while the other clawed at the wall beside her. She didn't even feel the pain of her fingernails snapping as she drew her hand toward her, leaving grooves in the wood paneling. Her heart beat so aggressively, it was as if it was trying to punch its way out of her chest. She felt it slam against her palm before shooting back against her spine.

All she could do was scream hysterically as her smiling mother stomped toward her, giggling happily as she flexed her long-fingered hands and approached her daughter.

"I dream of . . . *reclamation*!" Her voice became the wind. It was a long, shrieking howl that shattered Celeste's eardrums.

Celeste felt not only overwhelmed by her fear, by the manifestation of all her worldly traumas, she was plunged icily into a cold bath of physical torment as well. The sound of her mother's voice was like a blast of nuclear power. Celeste's face felt pushed against her skull, like she was standing right behind a jet engine—

And then she was awake.

Again.

This time, instead of vomiting, Celeste fell off the side of the bed and slammed harshly into the floor with an astonished yelp.

She lay frozen on the ground, her breath short.

The wind was no longer yelling at her. Outside, she could even hear birdsong.

She opened her eyes, half expecting to see her mother's distorted, nightmarish face hovering over her.

Instead, she saw a beam of dull sunlight pouring into the room from the window, lighting the ground beside her.

She turned over onto her back and studied her hands.

Her nails were unbroken. They actually looked cleaner and more even than she recalled them being. There was also, thankfully, no vomit smeared on her front.

It had been a dream.

All of it.

Bokrug, her mother, the empty cabin—all of it.

"Th-Theo?" she asked the stillness.

A spark of fear dashed through her in the silence.

Then, from downstairs, she heard a sudden shout and a swear.

She hurried downstairs, half expecting, again, to see her mother, holding him in her knobby hands and twisting his head off of his shoulders.

Instead, she found her boyfriend standing by the sink, washing a burned finger.

"Yer lucky. I nearly dropped breakfast," he said, pointing to the cast iron skillet.

Ignoring him, she surprised herself by jumping into his arms and squeezing him tightly.

"Whoa, what's this about?" he asked, patting her back with one hand while he kept the other under the running water.

In a rush, she told him.

C H A P T E R   S I X

After she finished describing her nightmare to Theo, she shoveled food into her mouth while he processed the story. Eventually, he spoke. By this point, all that was left on Celeste's plate were a few bits of egg and a small clump of hashbrowns. It looked like it had been a good and hearty breakfast, she thought, but she'd been too disturbed to taste any of it.

"It's never been so real before," Theo said.

"What was it like for you?" she asked.

"Not like that." Theo shook his head. "Last night, I dreamed I was in a succulent garden inside one of the caves. It was beautiful."

"Don't rub it in." It was surreal even joking about it, but she needed at least a wedge between herself and what she'd just experienced. At least, she thought, she wasn't sleepy. As mentally exhausting as her night had been, she couldn't envision closing her eyes and drifting back to sleep anytime soon.

"I'm sorry," Theo said.

Celeste set her utensils down and began to eat her hashbrowns with her fingers. "I just wish I'd been warned. If I knew how bad it could get—"

"It's never been like that before. For anyone," Theo said. "I've done this ritual over and over again. I was confident it was safe. Celeste, if I'd known, I never would have brought you here!"

Do I believe him? I think I do. But I want to look at all of this with a level head. I want to go home.

"After we eat, let's head out," she said, trying to sound casual, as if they'd already discussed it.

Theo flinched. "We can't."

"Theo, I'd like to go home." Her voice was firmer now. "I think after last night, I just need some time alone"—*Don't say that; if he is crazy, he'll take it as a threat*—"to get some real rest."

"No, Celeste . . . you don't understand—"

"Theo. I don't want to do this anymore."

"Celeste, I don't know if that's up to us."

She paused. "What do you mean?"

"I mean . . . look." He stood and went to the table where the goblet sat.

"I don't want to see that right now. I'll throw up," Celeste warned.

"No. Look." He brought the goblet to her.

It was clean. Celeste tried to remember if Theo had washed it out last night—and then she remembered her brief vision before they'd gone to bed. She'd thought it looked as if someone had drunk their mixture of fluids.

But he could have washed it this morning, right before making breakfast.

Besides, what did that prove about anything? So what the goblet was empty? It didn't compel her to stay here and experience more traumatic nightmares.

"What am I looking at, Theo?" she asked.

"It's begun. The ritual has already started. We built up to it before coming here, but putting ourselves in this cup and offering it to Bokrug . . . Once it starts, it won't end until Sunday night. Like we planned."

Celeste furrowed her brow. "I want to go home."

"I've never stopped the ritual before."

"Theo, this is crazy!"

"And Lavinia told me a ritual can't be stopped once it's begun. Bokrug . . . you *saw* him last night. Do you really think you can just drive away from that?"

Celeste's blood boiled. He hadn't warned her of the nightmares, sure, because he'd seemed unaware of how bad they could get. But he hadn't clarified to her that once started, this wouldn't end until it was seen through. Had he?

"You aren't telling me everything," she stated in a sharp tone.

Theo flinched again.

Celeste pointed. "There! You can't even hide it very well. What aren't you telling me?"

Theo swallowed. "I'm just scared. Celeste, I'm scared that if we leave, it'll just . . . follow us."

"Not us. Me."

Theo shook his head. "Us. We're its worshippers now. What Bokrug shows us in our dreams, it shows us for a reason."

Celeste's eyes widened. "You didn't tell me what it was. You told me to just close my eyes and think its name—*his* name."

He nodded. "We were praying. We gave him a sacrifice . . . and then we prayed to him. That's the ritual. You know what happens to gods no one prays to?"

Celeste shook her head.

"They grow small. They grow weak. There was a time in Earth's history were Bokrug was as big as you envisioned him. He could move the ocean and drown cities. But that time passed. A new kingdom was built where Ib once stood, and his idols and statues were tossed into the sea." Theo set the goblet down and went back to the table. He came back with the stone upon which a strange symbol had been scrawled. "I told you . . . this is a sign of doom. Do you know how I know that? Because Bokrug showed me . . . one of his last worshipers put it on the altar of a new god to remind people the Old Ones are still alive, even when they're forgotten."

"So . . . what? Is he harmless, or is he—"

"He should be harmless. Should be. But you . . . something about you brought more than a memory back to life. When I've performed the ritual, when Lavinia taught it to me, all that happened was what I expected you to see last night. Visions. The dreams are supposed to be conversational. You get shown places and people who no longer exist. That's it. You . . . Celeste, you woke him up."

She shuddered. "I didn't mean to. I didn't *want* to." Now, she felt a strange surge of guilt. Here she was, crying about being in the middle of a ritual she could have stopped herself before it had begun. But she'd wanted to support Theo. Wanted to be involved in what he was doing. And this, he'd told her, was the heart and soul of his passion.

There'd been no adequate warning, and it wasn't her fault for wanting to trust someone who seemed trustworthy. And yet her cheeks were flushed, and her eyes were bleary with new tears.

"I'm sorry," Theo said. "I can't take you back. I wish I could. But we have to see this through. The best you can do is surrender control. Let Bokrug show you what he wants. Then, when he's done, he'll let us go and—"

"How do you know that?"

"Because why would he want to scare off the only people left on Earth who are praying to him?"

It sounded reasonable, but when she closed her eyes, she saw the maiden falling, the green people crying from their caves as foamy seawater threatened to wash them away. Bokrug didn't seem to care much for his own people—and if he hadn't wanted to scare her, then why did he bring her to the void? Why had he tormented her with a ghoulish recreation of her mother?

Celeste felt like she was being twisted in multiple directions.

"I don't want to do this anymore, Theo. Isn't that enough?"

"No." His voice was firmer than before. "I won't risk it. If I take you home and something bad happens—"

"What if something bad happens here? Tonight? What if I fall asleep and . . ." She didn't want to even consider it. "She said she wanted to reclaim me. She said she dreams of hurting me."

"Your mother can't reach you here."

"How do you know? What if she . . . I don't know. What if she died and Bokrug found her? What if she's a witch now, and she's been performing this ritual? What if—"

"You don't know any of that. Did your mother ever have an interest in witchcraft or Magick?"

"No, but—"

"You said she was a Christian, didn't you?"

"Yes, but—"

"Christians don't do what we did, Celeste. They don't put their blood into goblets and worship ancient sea gods. They don't—"

"I haven't seen her since I was a kid, Theo! I don't *know* what she's been doing since then, and I don't want to know! I just don't want to see her again! Ever!" Celeste stood and crossed her arms. "I shouldn't have even come here after the first dream about her. It was a warning, wasn't it?"

Theo frowned.

"It was a warning. It was. You knew it. When I told you I'd dreamed about her, you knew it was a warning, and you went ahead and did the ritual anyways."

"I didn't know. I promise."

"Your promises don't mean much right now."

Theo's face fell. "Celeste, I'm trying to keep you safe."

"If you wanted to keep me safe, you wouldn't have had me spit in that awful thing." She knocked the goblet off the table, hoping it would shatter on the ground. It bounced and rolled instead.

"You're mad. I get it. I'd be mad too."

"Oh, please!" Celeste started toward the stairs.

"Where are you going?"

"To pack."

"For what? We can't leave."

"Theo . . . I don't care if you stay. I'm gone. I don't want anything else to do with this."

"It doesn't work that way."

"Then how does it work? Can you explain it, or are you just driving blind?"

"Celeste, please listen. I'm just as confused as you are."

"No, you aren't. I know I want to leave. There's no

confusion about it."

She knew, even as she said it, she was putting up a front. She was terribly, dreadfully confused. Part of her was seeking a rational answer or a quick solution. The other half knew rationality had no place here. Perhaps Theo was right and the only way to finish this was by letting it play out.

Theo stood by the dinner table, watching as she rounded the corner and went up the stairs. She felt bad yelling at him, but he'd put up his own sort of wall, which she'd have rather bulldozed than climbed over. All she wanted to do at the moment was complete a simple task, to feel like she was doing something rather than being pulled by invisible strings the way she'd been in her dream.

If I never dream again, I'll be happy for it, she thought as she went up the stairs and toward the bedroom.

Celeste slammed the door behind her, put her back to it, and covered her face in her hands. She had no tears left to shed, so she remained posed there, just letting her face get hot with her own breath as she waited for her heart to simmer down in her ribcage.

When, eventually, the rhythmic thump of her pulse was muted, she picked up her suitcase and unzipped it. At first, she tossed her clothes at the bed, not caring where or how they landed. When all of her sweaters and pants had become a mountain on the bed's edge, Celeste carefully folded and packed them.

She'd never been great with laundry (before coming here, she'd shoved her clothes haphazardly into her suitcase), but the process of folding each individual item gave her an opportunity to slow down and think.

Downstairs, she heard Theo washing the dishes. He was probably in a similar state, wondering what came next, what had really happened last night, and whether or not leaving was the right thing.

No, he's sure it isn't. There's not a doubt in his mind. Celeste squirmed as she folded a red cardigan. *Maybe you're both being pitted against each other. Why did the second nightmare begin with me in an empty bed? I also thought the footsteps coming up the steps were Theo's before the door opened and my mom came in.*

Maybe it wants me to leave.

But why would it want that?

It . . . or "he."

Bokrug.

She didn't even want to think about his terrible name. If praying to Bokrug gave him power, allowing him to occupy her mind would certainly fuel him further. But there was nothing she could do about it. Now that the name was in her brain, it circled around her like a whirling halo. She could see, just as clearly as she had in her nightmare, the impressive form of the beast-god floating out of the void and consuming her in one gulp.

Then a horrible thought occurred to her.

What if you're still dreaming?

She'd been so convinced she was awake after the dream about Bokrug. In fact, she'd been confident even when her elongated mother stormed into her room and came running toward her. It was clear magic dreams (if "magic" was the correct term, and she felt it wasn't) were craftier than regular ones. They were deceptive and confrontational, and you couldn't be sure what was real and what was fake when you were in them.

A cold chill crept down her spine, and her stomach became a rock tumbler.

This is how people go crazy, Celeste, her uncle's reasonable voice came to her. *They start to doubt reality. They can't tell the difference, eventually, between what's in your head and what's actually happening to you.*

But, she countered, *it did happen to me. It actually happened to me. I saw her again, and she was even worse than I remembered. She said she wanted to reclaim me.*

Again, she heard her mother's whispered words.

She wanted to tell herself she was being gullible and stupid. She'd let Theo's ideas get into her head and deform her thinking. The second she got away from this cabin, everything would make sense again and it would be as though she'd woken up from a long, terrible dream.

But she just couldn't believe it.

She'd finished packing her clothing and she hadn't even realized it. Folding each item had saved some space in her case, meaning she could have packed three more outfits if she'd wanted. But who needed to change clothes so often in one weekend?

Robotically, she began to unpack her clothing, putting them back where they'd been in the closet and in the sock drawer.

Just as the last sweater was going into the closet, she heard something scuttle beneath the bed. Celeste stood still, ears perked up.

"Hello?" she asked the empty room.

A small whisper leaked out from beneath the mattress.

Celeste backed away. "M-mom?" she asked.

There came no reply. Only a sound like cloth rubbing against cloth.

A furry rodent shot out from under the bed and raced toward the closet. Celeste clamped her hands over her mouth to stop herself from screaming. Just as her eyes focused on the blur, it was gone, vanished into the shadowy closet.

Just a rat. A big rat, but only a rat.

Any other day, she would have been sickened by the critter. Today, she was relieved. The rat posed little threat when compared to other monsters—

Celeste heard a knock on the bedroom door. Her blood froze, and her heart pumped like a piston. She's been so distracted by the rodent, she hadn't heard Theo's footsteps up the stairs.

"Hello?" she asked, worried it would be her

mother's voice responding or she'd open the door and a stream of rats would come racing into the room, swarming and chewing through her feet before she had a chance to kick them off. As the nightmare imagery grew more realistic in her head, her heart began to pick up speed. It felt like the organ was climbing up her throat with sharp-fingered hands.

"Hey," Theo said through the door.

"Hey," she responded, her voice so low she doubted he heard her. At once, the rat was forgotten. She went toward the door and held the knob, considering whether she would open it or not.

"I know you probably don't want to see me right now. But . . . there's something important I think you ought to come downstairs and look at."

She hesitated. "I'm just scared, Theo. I'm really scared."

"I know. I'm sorry. I shouldn't have—I don't know. I thought it was safe."

She believed him. God help her, she believed him.

"What is it you need me to see?" she asked.

"I think . . . I think someone came to the cabin while we were sleeping."

Another chill raced down her spine like an ice cube dropped down the back of her shirt.

"I think someone is messing with the ritual. I think that's what happened last night. We aren't doing this alone."

C H A P T E R   S E V E N

Packed in their winter clothes, Celeste and Theo braved the elements and stood on the back porch, looking at the symbol. Painted beside the sliding glass door in broad, sloppy strokes, whoever had left the mark had been in a hurry. The crimson paint had frozen, but it still looked drippy and wet. Celeste thought it wasn't paint but was actually fresh blood. She couldn't stop herself from thinking of the jagged, cherry-red line her dream-self had cut across the circle in the woods.

"That's the same symbol, isn't it?" Celeste asked. "The one from your rock?"

He didn't have to say it. They were both thinking it.

Doom.

"I already checked the cabin. I didn't see anyone," Theo explained.

"Is there a basement?"

"No. No. God no." Theo turned toward the woods and studied the bare trees. She followed his gaze and watched the forest that surrounded them, wondering if she'd see a fleeting shadow or a blatant figure standing just within the trees, waving creepily at them the way ghosts did in horror movies.

The wind made the trees sway like seaweed caught in a current. The storm was becoming much more intense than predicted, but maybe that, too, had something to do with the archaic symbol scrawled on the cabin's side. At this point, Celeste could believe anything was possible.

"It's my mother," she found herself saying. Already, she wished she could shove the words back into her mouth and swallow them, but they couldn't be taken back. "I don't know how, but she found us. She followed us. She's—she's controlling this."

"It can't be her." Theo shook his head.

"How do you know?"

"It's impossible. It just is."

"How do you know?"

He set his jaw. "Oh, Christ. I had . . . I had Rich look her up."

Celeste's face paled.

"I don't know why. I shouldn't have. But I never knew what happened to Lavinia. She just vanished and—and I thought if I could get some closure for you, it would make me feel better. If I knew what had happened to her. It was selfish and stupid, and I regretted it immediately."

She didn't want his apologies. "Where is she, Theo?" she asked bluntly.

"Your mother died three years ago."

Celeste didn't know what to say. She'd cut all ties to the woman who'd birthed her and had even legally changed her last name. There was no way she was marked as "next of kin" in her mother's emergency contacts either.

Still, she was surprised no one had notified her. But then, who was going to connect the dots? It wasn't like Celeste's mother was going to leave her anything in her will. The only person who would have cared to tell her was her uncle, Lucas, who had died unfairly before the hag had.

"How?" she asked meekly.

Theo didn't meet her eyes when he responded. "Rich said she . . . committed suicide."

Celeste imagined the woman dangling from the rafters of her attic, bedsheets tied securely around her throat, her face blue and swollen.

Celeste shook the vision away and repeated herself. "How?"

Theo mustered up the words with visible effort. "Rich said he had to ask some of the local police. No one wanted to talk about it."

"What did she do?"

"She starved herself to death. She locked herself in her house and just . . . let herself die."

It was even worse than the death Celeste had pictured. Now, she saw a raw, skeletal body laying stiff on a bed, emaciated and agonized, her eyes turned different directions and her mouth yawning open, exposing a fence-like line of blocky teeth—

And then she was back in the bedroom, screaming as her mother came toward her, arms outstretched, fingers cracking as they twiddled. Each footstep was a detonation, each word a whispered scream—

"It's her."

"Celeste, your mother is dead."

"So are all those people in Ib, but I saw them last night." She crossed her arms. "My mother is here. I know it. I can feel it."

Theo picked at his words like they would bite him if he misspoke. "Celeste, these dreams don't raise the dead. We're watching Bokrug's memories. We aren't—we aren't bringing Ib back. No one can do that."

"What happened to Ib? How do the dreams end?" Celeste asked.

Theo shrugged.

"All these dreams, and you don't know?"

"I know they died. That's it. I know the entire city was wiped off the face of the earth. The rock I brought with me is all that's left over."

Celeste pictured a deluge. A flood of biblical proportions. Maybe the flood that inspired that particular story to begin with, mistaken as an act of God when really it was Bokrug's wrath. And for what? Did the green people eventually run out of maidens?

"I think we should go inside," Theo said.

Celeste snapped around and looked again toward the woods. She expected to see her nine-foot-tall mother crawling out from the tree line on all fours. Instead, she was greeted with a blinding blast of fresh snow. The wind was becoming agitated. It felt like she was being punched in the gut and slapped in the face with it.

"The storm is getting worse," Theo said. "I'd rather we talked about this inside." He sounded like he was on the verge of panicking.

"Okay," Celeste relented before taking one last gander at the symbol.

A circle with a jagged line stitched across it, with tendrils blooming from its sides. It looked like a blob of dropped blood, frozen mid-splash. When she'd been in college, her roommate had been a psych major. For fun, she'd once brought a stack of Rorschach tests back to their dorm, and they spent the night joking around with them, diagnosing themselves and each other with ridiculous fake mental diseases in response to their increasingly bawdy responses to the question: "When you look at this, what do you see?" Celeste had never taken the scrambled images seriously enough to give her roommate an honest answer. But gazing upon the last symbol left behind by Bokrug's people, Celeste now saw many terrible things.

Theo took her by the hand and tugged her toward the door, back into the warmth of their cabin. The second her eyes were pulled away from the symbol, relief washed over her. It was like she'd forgotten how to breathe without even noticing she was in danger of suffocating. The air rushed into her lungs and kickstarted her heart.

Theo slid the door closed and then released a hearty sigh. She didn't have to ask him; she knew he'd felt the same. As if something icier than the snow had taken hold of them.

Theo shuffled out of his coat and snow shoes, leaving wet puddles on the floor. Celeste followed suit. Afterwards, she sat on the sofa and waited for him to make tea.

They didn't speak until after their mugs were half-emptied and the steam had dissipated entirely.

"It will follow us, won't it?" Celeste asked.

Theo grimaced into his mug. "Yes. I think it will. Lavinia kept me in the dark about a few things, but she made it very clear a ritual like this can't be stopped once it's started."

"Why didn't you warn me?"

"Because it's never been harmful before. Ever. I mean it; I've never once even had a nightmare while performing the Dream Cycle."

"So . . . it's me, isn't it? Something about me brought this out."

"No. We both saw the symbol. There's someone else here, and they're—"

"It's my mother," Celeste stated resolutely. "I know it is. I brought her ghost here. Somehow, the ritual gave her—I don't know. Power? Control?"

"It's not that type of ritual. It's not your mother. It's Bokrug. He's had access to your memories, just like you've had access to his, and he made you see your mother. But it wasn't her. Not really. It just—" He waved a hand. "It just looks like her."

Celeste thought. She wasn't sure whether or not any of what he'd said made sense, but she had no counterarguments, so she was willing to accept it for the moment.

"What if we stay awake? What if we just drink coffee and stay up all weekend, and then we can leave and—"

"And go to sleep in your own bed, where Bokrug will be waiting for you? It's a ritual that's supposed to take place over three nights, but it doesn't have to be three nights in a row. The only thing staying up will do is exhaust us."

Celeste set her cup down and crossed her arms. "Well, I don't imagine falling asleep tonight anyways."

"Maybe we sleep in shifts? We can wake each other up if it looks like things are getting bad."

"How will we know? Did I wake you up last night?"

"No."

"When you got up to make breakfast, did I look like I was going through hell?"

"You were sleeping peacefully," he admitted. "Your eyes were fluttering a bit, but I just assumed you were having an active dream."

"That's an understatement."

"Okay. So . . . I don't know. Maybe there's something we can do to stop this from getting any worse, but I don't know what it is." He paused.

Celeste closed her eyes. They felt dangerously weary. Despite what she'd said, she didn't feel rested after last night, and what she wanted more than anything was to lay down and drift away. But the fear of where she'd drift to forced her to open her eyes and dig her nails into her left arm. It did little to quash the fatigue, but at least she was awake.

"Celeste?" Theo asked.

"I don't know what to do," Celeste said. "I'm just scared."

"Celeste . . ." There was something *wrong* with his voice.

She turned toward him—

Theo's eyes were bleeding tears. His mouth was stuck in a yawn, and it was like a faucet had been opened in his skull. Thick, oily water poured freely from his mouth. It spattered soundlessly on his lap, throwing droplets in all directions.

"Celeste, come back," he said in a whisper, his lips unmoving. "*Come back to Ib.*"

Celeste stood and screamed.

Theo jumped to his feet, took her by the arms, and held her still before she had a chance to run.

"What's wrong? Celeste, what did you see?" Theo asked.

She stopped another shriek from leaving her when

she realized Theo's face was returned to normal, his lap was dry, and there had really been no water at all.

"Did I fall asleep?" she asked.

"Maybe. I don't know. I was talking and you just kind of—you froze. Then you screamed. What happened?" Theo asked.

"I saw—oh, God!" She began to shake with tears.

CHAPTER EIGHT

Celeste tried to focus on anything but the dreams, the symbol, and Bokrug. Unfortunately, there was nothing else to do in the cabin. They'd brought books to read. Celeste tried picking up a thriller by Harlan Coben. A lot of her friends in the English department tended to look down on popular books, but Celeste loved them as much as she did the classics. In fact, she ardently defended them (especially those works targeting a female demographic, which were often dismissed outright without having been read).

In her opinion, Harlan Coben was one of the best there was. Regrettably, the present circumstances prevented her from escaping into the story.

She read the opening line on repeat but couldn't retain it. She tried just barreling through and taking in a full paragraph, but at the end, she realized she didn't even know whether the book was in first or third person. She decided to try at least reading the reviews in the front pages, where the *New York Times* lauded Coben's work. Even those were tricky for her. Between the words, she saw long gaps of blank space, and her ears rang like an old TV had been broken and all the static inside was then poured into her skull.

She shut *I Will Find You* and set it aside. Instinctually, she began to do what she did at home when she didn't feel motivated. She lay back on the sofa and shut her eyes.

She sat bolt upright, remembering Theo's fountaining eyes from the last time she'd nodded off.

I'll have no choice. I need to go to sleep sometime.

She checked out the wall clock above the fireplace. It was four in the afternoon. The day had bled away from her. Time was moving simultaneously too fast and too slow.

"Are you hungry?" Theo asked, coming down the stairs.

"No. Not really."

"We should eat anyways. We skipped lunch."

"What were you doing up there?" she asked.

"I was resting."

She nearly leapt to her feet. "What happened?"

"Nothing. It was a void dream. I kept expecting to see Bokrug, like you did . . . but nothing happened." He watched his feet. "I considered not telling you."

"Could be a good sign. Maybe it means he's done—" She sought the words but couldn't find them.

"I don't think so," Theo said, more to himself than to his girlfriend. He trudged into the kitchen and went to work. Even in the midst of a crisis, he took his time to make their dinner right.

Celeste drew in the energy to set the table. Nothing fancy, but she made sure they were both sat close to each other. She did believe him, that none of this was intentional, but she didn't want to say it aloud yet. She wanted to know for sure rather than just in her heart. Still, she saw the table placement as a sort of peace offering and hoped he'd recognize it.

They had salmon on rice with a dash of soy sauce each and a side of greens. It was a healthy and delicious meal, but Celeste couldn't appreciate it. Especially when she inhaled the scent of fish and was brought back to the shore by Ib, where the sea breeze was pungent and the waves were hard.

Afterwards, they stacked their plates in the sink. Celeste knew they ought to be washed right away, but neither she nor Theo seemed to have the gumption for it.

It was six, and the sun had fallen. She and Theo sat in the living room and listened to the wind, the creaking of the cabin, and the rustling of the naked trees. It was like a stampede of wolves surrounding them—threatening and braying.

Celeste could feel an invisible line pulling at her brain, urging her to lay down and rest. It would be unavoidable, she knew. The longer she tried to stay awake, the worse it would get.

"I'm sorry," Theo suddenly said, shocking her out of her thoughts. "This is really all my fault."

Celeste shook her head. "You didn't know."

"But I shouldn't have been messing with this stuff.

It's like . . . I wanted to claim some of what Lavinia did for myself. I should have just buried it."

"You didn't know," Celeste repeated.

Theo began to cry. Like most men, he swallowed the tears for as long as he could before they broke through.

Despite everything, Celeste wanted to be with him. She stood, walked over to his seat, and squeezed herself beside him. Slowly and tenderly, she draped her arms over him and pulled him close, letting his tears wet her chest.

They held and comforted each other, him rocking her in his arms, her hands drawing circles on his back and through his hair. Time ticked away and the wind howled for attention, but all Celeste could focus on was Theo.

"It's not your fault."

"No. It is—"

"What Lavinia did to you wasn't your fault."

Her words struck with the force of a chisel. She heard his breath still and felt his heart beat against her.

"It wasn't your fault, Theo," she repeated, her voice a lullaby.

He sniffled. She felt his grip around her tighten. A silent admission that he understood her but was unwilling to say so aloud.

She felt stupid for having doubted him, for having been so combative all day. At the same time, she'd been thrust into something she hadn't been prepared for. Could never have been ready for, even if Theo *had* known to warn her. And like him, she understood what it meant to reclaim something that had once belonged intrinsically to an abuser.

As she aged, Celeste knew she looked like her mother. She had the same eyes, the same sharp nose, and the same faded, grey freckles. She worried, as she began the process of medical transitioning, she wasn't finding her own identity but was in fact recreating her hateful, abusive mother out of her own body. This thought was twisted around and became something even worse. She worried she was only transitioning out of spite, because it was something her mother had accused her of being before she'd truly known it herself. She spent many days fretting over the idea that becoming the woman she had always seen herself to be was actually a backfired act of reverse psychology, the way some fathers forced their girls to play sports because they'd wanted a boy.

It had hurt a lot, this process of deconstructing the web of hatred her mother had ensnared her within. She'd been beaten so many times, eventually it felt like that was indeed what she deserved. And there were days where she blamed herself for not being the son her mother wanted, for being a disappointment to someone she didn't even love.

On these occasions, when she voiced her worries, Uncle Lucas had to tell her (even when he knew she wasn't receiving the words) that what her mother had done was evil, and she was guiltless, and she was fulfilling a promise to herself when she decided to transition.

You aren't becoming what your mother hated. You're becoming what you are.

The abuses Theo had suffered were different. He'd been tricked into becoming a servant to a woman who'd believed herself a witch, and she'd used the powers she convinced him he was gaining to trick him into rituals no little child should have witnessed, much less participated in. The specifics were still unknown to Celeste, and she wasn't about to wheedle them out of Theo, especially when he was as vulnerable as he was in this moment.

But she'd heard enough to know the rituals had been sexual and violent. Lavinia had also made young Theo bring her animals from the neighborhood, and eventually, the responsibility became his to kill them as well. She'd put her talons in him when he was too young to recognize the differences between fact and fiction, and she'd convinced him (methodically) what they were doing was normal. That every house in America had a room where Old Gods were worshipped and it was Theo's parents who were strange because they hadn't such a room in their home.

When he eventually told his parents what he'd been doing when he went to Lavinia's house, he had been more shocked that *they* were shocked.

The thought made Celeste's heart sore.

She didn't blame him for wanting one ritual for his own. She was only sorry now that even that had been ruined for him. Her involvement had (somehow) taken a beautiful and peaceful ritual and had twisted it into a horror show.

The truth was Celeste felt as guilty as Theo did. She wanted him to tell her it wasn't her fault as well. Both of them were once brainwashed into believing lies about themselves.

For Celeste, she'd believed she was supposed to be someone she wasn't, complying to what others saw rather than what she felt was true in her heart.

For Theo, it was what Lavinia tricked him into thinking. She convinced him he wasn't being abused. What she was making him do with her was "special" and even "magical" rather than horrifying.

Celeste held him close, compressing him against her.

"I love you," he said. Simple words, but they'd never felt so poignant.

"I love you too," she replied.

"I'm sorry."

"You don't have to be."

"I just feel . . . I feel so fucked-up about it."

She shushed him. "It's not your fault. What she did was wrong."

Theo closed his eyes so tight, it was as if he wanted his face to cave in. "I remember how my parents told me not to talk about it. But word spread. Some of my friends liked to joke about it. They said I should count myself lucky. That I'd gotten laid before any of them. They asked what it was like and were shocked when I didn't answer the way they thought I would. They just couldn't understand that I hadn't enjoyed it."

She'd have needed to have broken her own skin to hold him any closer.

"I think about it constantly. And every time I've come out here, I hope I'm insulting her. I'm making this thing my own, and she can't control it the way she used to."

"I understand," she said.

"You think it's your mother doing this . . . I think it's Lavinia. She found me. I think she's in the woods watching us. And I feel so guilty because I never wanted her to know you existed, Celeste. I didn't want anyone so horrible to even know your name. But I brought you right to her. I . . . I gave you to her, and I didn't even realize I was doing it."

She didn't know how to respond. Part of her thought it was ridiculous, but it wasn't any more ridiculous than her own theories.

The last little bit of her rationality died there. It was drowned in Theo's tears.

Oh, God, I wish we'd never come here, she thought.

The notion curdled Celeste's blood, but it had to be considered. After everything, she didn't know if she could doubt it, even if she tried.

What if Lavinia was watching their cabin from the forest, laughing as they wept, cooking up more bad dreams in her witch's cauldron?

The wicked bitch could very well be the cause of their troubles.

There came an abrupt knock at the front door, which shocked both of them to attention.

C H A P T E R   N I N E

Celeste and Theo watched the front door. The Klaxon wail of the wind had increased outside, roaring through the mountain. They could see a dim shape standing just in front of the door through the frosted glass, but neither could make anything specific out about the figure. Man or woman, human or . . . something else. All they could see was a blob of shadow that shifted every once in a while like it was tired of standing.

"Wh-what do we do?" Celeste asked.

"I don't know," Theo said. His hands were cinched into fists, and he'd wiped his tears away.

The knocking came again. It was loud and firm.

"It knows we're here. We can't hide from it," Celeste said.

"But we don't have to let it in."

No. He was right. At the same time, not knowing what was on the other side of the door was somehow worse. Celeste wished there was a peephole she could look through.

"The bedroom," Theo whispered.

"What?"

"I could look out the bedroom window and onto the porch. Maybe see who we're dealing with."

"Okay." Celeste nodded. "It's the best we can do, isn't it?"

Together, they walked toward the door. Both moved cautiously, as if they worried the wrong footstep would usher the figure in—whether the door was locked or not.

When the wood floor creaked under Celeste's feet, she clamped a hand over her mouth and froze in place. Gently, she took her next step on tiptoes.

They entered the bedroom, side by side. She was reminded of their first hours in the cabin. Before the nightmares, things had been cheery and bright. She wished they could go back to that mood, but the atmosphere at the cabin had been irrevocably altered. Celeste didn't know if it could ever be reverted, even if they safely made it through their stay. After the Dream Cycle was over, Celeste considered burning the place down, just in case any part of Bokrug remained.

Theo crept toward the window and parted the curtains with two fingers. He peered out. When he let the curtains fall closed, he wore a confused expression.

"Who is it?" Celeste asked.

"It's . . ."

"Who?" she repeated when he failed to finish his sentence.

"It's a king."

"What do you mean?"

"Look for yourself." He held the curtain open.

Celeste looked out the window, nearly smudging the glass with her nose.

Theo hadn't been lying, but he hadn't painted the whole picture for her.

It was indeed a creature dressed like a king . . . but it wasn't a human being.

The figure was seven feet tall and stooped so low he appeared to have a hunchback. He wore purple robes and a tall crown made from discarded pieces of coral. His eyes were chunky, featureless, and solid, like coal. He had no mouth below his rounded nose, just a flat slate of skin that looked like wood varnishing. Despite that, he'd grown an impressive beard that stretched down to his ankles. It was as white as the snow flurries that beat at his humped back.

She watched as one of his crooked, three-fingered fists rose and knocked again on the door. He lowered his arm, and it vanished within his robes. Patiently, he waited, tilting on his feet in the breeze.

"What . . . is he?" she asked.

"I don't know," Theo said. "I've never seen anything like him before."

The king's head turned toward them.

Celeste let the curtains fall closed. She backed away from the window, heart thudding. She and Theo both stood still, waiting for something terrible to happen, for the window to burst apart and for the weird king to step into their cabin and grab them both.

When three minutes had passed, Theo walked toward the window once again.

"No, Theo . . . don't," Celeste warned.

He peeked through the curtains. His shoulders fell with relief.

"Is he gone?" she asked.

"No. But he hasn't moved."

She heard a knock at the door again.

"If he wanted to break in . . . he could have," Theo said. "I don't think . . . I don't *feel* like he wants to hurt us."

"You don't know that."

"Maybe he wants to talk."

"He doesn't have a mouth."

Theo squinted. "Oh. You're right. I didn't notice that before."

"What's he doing now?"

"He's putting something on the door. He's . . . he's got some sort of chalk with him. He's—oh my god." Theo turned and dashed out of the bedroom.

Before Celeste could comprehend what was happening, she heard the front door swing open.

"Wait!" she shouted, vaulting out of the bedroom and into the narrow hallway. She thought Theo had gone mad. Why on Earth would he open the door for such a creature? Even if the thing meant them no harm, there was no way of knowing that until it was too late.

Celeste froze at the doorway, looking at her boyfriend and the towering king, who loomed over Theo without threatening him. Instead, the creature reached in so it could finish its scrawling.

It was drawing the symbol on the doorway.

The same symbol that had been etched into the last stone left over from Ib.

The same symbol that had been painted beside their back door.

The same symbol that Celeste had unknowingly cut through the circle in the woods during her dream.

This creature was responsible for it.

Her blood felt ignited as she took the lead, coming up toward the creature and demanding an answer. She pointed at the drawing and shouted, "What does it mean?"

The creature turned its narrow, wooden head toward her. Its eyes were incapable of blinking. Somehow, she felt it was trying to convey sorrow, despite the immobility of its bizarre face.

"What does it mean?" Celeste insisted.

Theo repeated her, just as insistent.

The creature returned its arm to the folds of its robes. It stooped lower, as if bowing.

They heard its voice in their heads.

"Taran-Ish."

Celeste raced toward the king. She grabbed his robes in her hands and held his eyes in her own, no longer caring if she was putting herself in danger.

"Please. Please stop this. We just want to go home. Whatever we did to upset you, please—"

"Not . . . me."

She was shocked to hear English, but it wasn't *exactly* like the creature was speaking to her. It was putting its thoughts into her head, allowing her brain to process them in her preferred tongue. They were images translated to words, like hieroglyphics. There was no tone or infliction to the voice. No individuality. It was blunt and clear, and that was all it needed to be.

"Taran-Ish . . . is not a conjuring sign. It . . . is a warning." He sighed deeply, a sound that reminded Celeste of lonely whales and saddened dogs. "It was . . . a warning . . . I, too, ignored . . ."

The king pulled away from her, turned, and started down the steps.

"Wait!" Celeste stepped onto the porch after him.

"Celeste, wait . . ." Theo said.

"No! He knows what's happening! *Wait*!" she cried.

"Celeste!"

She went into the snow, following the creature's footsteps. Rapidly, the king moved through the storm, allowing it to consume him. Every step he took faded him from sight.

Celeste didn't have time to put on shoes and a

jacket; she needed answers, and she knew this creature had them.

"Stop! Please! I need to know what's happening!" Celeste wailed.

"You will follow me," the voice returned to her. When it spoke, it was all she heard. Even the wind was dampened by it. "And I will show you my kingdom. Mighty Sarnath, which was built upon the bones of Ib."

The snow began to part much like stage curtains. The king ambled through the storm and vanished into the darkness beyond. Even though she could no longer see him, Celeste heard his voice. It drifted toward her through a haze.

"I am . . . the Olden King, Zokkar. It is a name I thought all would remember. It is a name long forgotten. There were, in my time, great gardens filled with strange and otherworldly fruit. The land prospered, and we could grow upon it whatever we desired."

Celeste found herself no longer walking through snow. Her freezing bare feet were warmed by wet, squelching moss. She stumbled from the shocking change, stalling only to catch her bearings before she realized she was standing in a garden.

"W-wait," she said, beholding a fantastic sight. "Where are we?"

"Sarnath," the king's voice came to her, drifting down from the sunlit sky like a sunbeam. She blinked away tears, her eyes stung by the brilliant sight of the sun. She hadn't realized it, but after the day she'd had, she'd never actually expected to see the sun again.

Sarnath.

This was, she realized, a garden built upon the shore where once Ib had stood. The entire cliff had been flattened, and now there was a long beach that stretched out toward the wilderness. There were no caves left, only mighty white towers built from a substance as clean and smooth as ivory. The tallest of which was multi-spired and was patrolled by sturdy guards with pointed spears. They, like their king, Zokkar, were mouthless, bearded, and all had coal-dark eyes.

The garden was filled with strange plants. Bulbous fruits sprouted from rope-thick stalks, which dangled from breathing trees. Ahead of her, she spotted a thorny-mouthed flytrap the size of a pizza box, and at her feet, there were crowded succulents, each of which was sheened in dripping fluid, like each one had become a spurting teat. She knew she could drink from them, and it would be better and more intoxicating than any liquor she'd had on Earth—

This isn't another planet. It's Earth before man.

She looked behind her, expecting to see a wall of snow. Maybe she could call Theo in, just so he could see how beautiful the city of Sarnath was—

But all she saw were more towers, more of the sandy, shell-littered beach, and the gentle waves of a tamed ocean. All she saw was more Sarnath.

Theo, why didn't you follow me?

She worried he had. What if he was lost in the

snow, calling her name as he plunged further and further into the cold? She was helpless to help him, just as he was helpless to find her.

"We scraped the kingdom of Ib from Earth. We tore down its primitive temples and replaced them with seventeen of our own. The least of which were mightier than any in Thraa or Ilarnek, or Kadatheron." Zokkar's voice overwhelmed her.

She followed the voice, weaving through the plants that bloomed throughout the crowded garden. They became odder as she went, and more organic. Some looked like flexing organs and tubes of living intestine woven through flower patches. Others were larger than her and shuddered as she walked past them, as if they wanted to lurch toward her and were resisting their baser urges.

She walked toward the heavily guarded temple, knowing she would be allowed entrance at Zokkar's behest. The guards watched her with their blank eyes, but none raised their spears or demanded she halt. They simply observed her the way she did them.

"It was our hubris that killed us. We cast Bokrug away from our kingdom and replaced him with our own gods. Lesser gods. Younger gods," Zokkar continued.

She saw no doorway into the temple. Only sheer walls as smooth and as pale as paper. She came upon the wall and followed it around the circumference of the temple. At last, she found a hole blown into the building's side. It looked like a cave's mouth and led down a thin, featureless tunnel.

Following her feet, she went down the tunnel and into the temple. Again, no guard made a move to stop her. She felt their eyes upon her, even after she was out of their sight.

The tunnel tightened and lowered. Soon, Celeste was crawling on her hands and knees, groaning with effort as she wormed her way toward her destination. Zokkar said nothing, but she could feel his presence in her skull as if he was resting within her like a comforted houseguest.

The walls became closer and bumpier, as if frozen fists were trying to impede her. She had to angle her shoulders sideways and squeeze through the obstructions, groaning with the effort. The breath squeezed out of her, and, bruises forming in her abdomen, she started to wiggle limblessly, like a fish working its way back to a stream from dry land. Then, with gasping relief, she was suddenly through the tunnel. The floor she collapsed onto was ice cold, bringing back memories of the snowy mountains. She remained on the ground only for a moment, knowing that even if she pinched her eyes shut and tried to rest, she couldn't.

You can't dream inside a dream. Not by choice, at least.

She was thankful to stand upright. It felt as if she'd been reborn after traveling through the rocky birth cannel. But now, she felt there was too much space around her. The cathedral was bigger on the inside than on the outside. She'd entered a building which reminded her of medieval castles and sturdy fortresses, but had crawled her way into a church the size of a football stadium.

It was a tall, domed room, whiter than the exterior and just as smooth. Featureless save for a massive, bony throne, which was defined by its shadows. The throne's back reached for the ceiling, ending with a crown of animal tusks. The armrests looked like elephant trunks, and they both curved inwards at their ends so they appeared rounded.

On either side of the throne were two beasts, fashioned by immaculately gifted hands. They were carved from stone, but the stone had been painted a ghastly gold. The animal effigies were hairless wolves with long snouts and fearsome eyes. Their teeth were jeweled, and their forked tongues hung like laundry from their mouths.

Each statue was exact in detail, totally identical to each other. They were both as tall as churches, dwarfing the king who sat on his throne between them.

The symbol of Taran-Ish was carved on the left beast's leg.

Taran-Ish.

A warning from Ib's high priest, who was executed by Zokkar in front of the remains of his people. He was beaten with one of the last statues of Bokrug, which hadn't yet been cast into the sea. She didn't know how she knew any of this. It was just there in her head, like a childhood memory rediscovered. In a similar fashion, she knew the statue had been put on display in the town's square, where it was spat upon and ridiculed by the people of Sarnath.

Taran-Ish was a priest (and I heard his voice when I watched the maiden sacrifice herself to Bokrug, didn't I?) . . . now, he is a warning. A symbol for doom to come.

"Yes . . ." Zokkar said as he peeled his crown away from his skull and set it on the armrest of his throne. "A warning I did not heed. When we destroyed Ib, we celebrated."

Celeste saw a table appear in the middle of the cathedral. It appeared without being carried in, as if it'd been invisible before and the spell had just worn off.

The table was crowded with tall creatures. They'd all taken their bearded masks off, exposing their real faces beneath and their hot, angry eyes, which had before been shielded by coal-black coverings. Their faces were skinless, wet, and red as sunburn. They looked hideous without their masks, and their real beards were stringy, wiry, and ill-kept. Each face looked like a sore, each mouth a vortex of shattered glass. They spoke to each other in raspy growls, knocking their glasses together before slurping down drinks derived from succulent plants from Zokkar's garden. Some brought in bulbous fruits, which they crushed in their three-fingered claws, gobbling up whatever fluids sprayed forth before discarding the skins and leaving them to be stomped onto the temple's floor.

It was like watching a herd of barbarians pillage their own village. Gone was any sense of nobility and grandeur. Especially when one of Zokkar's people stood up on the table and urinated into his friends' goblets. They drank greedily and happily, relishing in their own filth.

A smell like animal sewage hit Celeste, burning her eyes and stinging her nose. She realized several of the brutish dinner guests had defecated on their chairs, too enraptured by their drinks to even leave the table.

"When we destroyed Ib, we celebrated," Zokkar repeated from his throne as he lifted his mask and revealed his infected face. His eyes ran with yellowed goo, and his mouth seemed to fall from his skull, the lips torn and tattered and the teeth rotten green.

Celeste wanted to turn and run, but she couldn't. She was frozen in place, watching in terror as the dinner guests became louder and crueler.

One of the creatures was strangling another on the table. The beast cried for mercy as his friends cheered his killer on. Just as the creature was about to die, the grip of his assailant relented. He was then rolled off the table and forced to crawl on his hands and knees while the others chanted and pounded their fists on the drink- and filth-stained table.

The entire party was distracted when four green-skinned people came from around the throne, walking peacocks by leather leashes.

The chanting changed, becoming wilder and faster.

The enslaved remains of Ib seemed embarrassed to be seen. They were naked, beaten, and shackled together. Grey blood seeped from their fresh wounds, leaving dots on the white floor.

The peacocks were beautiful. Their tails fanned out behind them, ornate and colorful. Each peacock was bigger than any bird Celeste had seen at the zoo. Their heads were wider, with flattened bills instead of beaks. Celeste wished she had a camera because she knew she'd never be able to accurately describe their majesty to Theo.

Two of Bokrug's people had to struggle to lift a heavy bird from the floor. They dropped the beast on the table, where it struggled to stay on its feet and flap its weighty wings.

Instantly, the skinless creatures swarmed the first of the peacocks.

Celeste wanted to scream as she watched the people tear it to pieces before her frightened eyes.

They dug their claws in and ripped shredded flesh and patches of glossy feathers away. The bird released a mournful shriek before its head was yanked from its neck. Its beak was pried open like a book, splitting its multicolored head in half.

From his throne, Zokkar held out his hands, palms up, as two of Bokrug's people brought him a bird of his own. They set the creature on his lap and then ducked away, standing as far from his throne and from the banquet table as they were permitted to be.

It flapped its wings once, but Zokkar grabbed ahold of it and throttled it by the throat, breaking its neck so its head hung limply from his fist. Then he turned it over and speared its chest with his sharpened fingers.

Celeste closed her eyes and wept. She could hear the bird's blood falling from the throne and trickling down toward the table, staining the white cathedral's immaculate floor.

Zokkar gathered the bird's steaming organs and shoveled them raw into his mouth. He chewed brazenly, devouring the bird's innards.

When Celeste opened her eyes, she saw two of his followers kneeling by his sides, collecting the streaming blood in goblets. When they were filled, they lifted the cups to Zokkar's lips so he could drink as he chewed.

The people from Ib stood in attendance, heads bowed, eyes draining tears. Peacock blood spattered their faces and chests. Celeste knew they would have wanted to wipe the fluids away, but they were not permitted to. They had been instructed to stand and watch as the magnificent birds were torn, defiled, and devoured in front of them.

"When we destroyed Ib, we celebrated," Zokkar said again.

The table was gone. So were the birds, the dinner guests, and the enslaved people of Ib. The smells had also vanished. The coppery scent of blood and the swampy odor of bodily waste was replaced with overwhelming sterility, as if Zokkar had wanted the temple cleansed of sin and degradation.

Zokkar remained on his throne, but he'd aged.

In an eye-blink, he'd turned crooked and knotted, and his breath seeped out of his melting mouth in wheezy, painful strokes. He clutched the arms of his throne with pale hands, each wrinkle a deep groove. His eyes were deflated and milky, the yellow infections replaced with gelatinous tears.

"Sarnath . . . was built on a grave . . . and we . . . we danced . . . we danced upon it . . ."

The golden monsters by his sides began to tilt. They seemed repulsed by their dying king and wanted to run away from him.

"We danced . . . and we danced . . . and we danced . . ."

The left fell over. It shattered like glass when it hit the ground, sending black ink and shards of gold in all directions.

"We prayed to our gods, but they were weak. Bokrug . . . consumed them."

The wolf on the right toppled, breaking just as his brother had.

"We prayed then, to Bokrug. But he . . . showed us . . . no mercy!"

Zokkar's mouth burst open, and water flowed forth. It smelled of brine and splashed harshly onto the floor in a sweeping wave. The wave gathered mass and then rose toward Celeste. She stumbled backward, knowing there was no escape even before it crashed upon her, dashing her into the floor. She felt a spark of agony as her head hit the solid ground. There was a blurt of white light that lasted only a second before she was returned to consciousness.

The water tossed her back and forth. Celeste

struggled to stay awake as the wave filled her mouth and inflated her lungs.

She clawed toward the surface, but she was no longer in the king's cathedral. After the wave had hit her, the entire environment had once again changed.

She was in the sea.

The city of Sarnath was sunken beneath her kicking legs. Miles and miles below, it had been drowned by a deluge of ocean water. Bloated corpses floated up from the toppled towers and flooded houses. Their false beards trailed after them as they rose toward the surface, making each body look like flotsam. Some of Sarnath's people were struggling to swim, entrapped in their own tangled beards and cumbersome robes.

"We were doomed . . . doomed to drown . . . doomed by the Old God Bokrug."

She watched the city begin to dissolve as though it was being doused not in water but in acid.

Some of the bodies broke apart and disintegrated, swallowed up by sudden shadows that floated through the sea like ink-black jellyfish. It was like watching cancerous polyps devour blood cells. Terrible, sucking, formless mouths closed over flailing bodies before they could lift themselves toward the heavens. Bodies rose, but none broke free.

Those that weren't instantly swallowed were dragged into mouths by twisted tentacles, which ensnared kicking limbs and tightened around bucking torsos.

Celeste kicked harder, forcing herself toward the surface. Glittery spears of sunlight broke through the thrashing waves above, promising warmth and safety.

She wasn't going to allow herself to be sucked back into Bokrug's void. She'd seen enough of him, enough of Sarnath, and enough of Zokkar and his regrets.

She fought in screaming terror for air, but her lungs weighed her down. They'd been filled like sandbags, and she was being drawn backwards toward the sunken city.

No! No! Please! I don't want to die here! I don't deserve it! I didn't do anything wrong! I didn't— please! Please! I'm begging you! I just want to live—

She broke out of the snow and screamed.

Theo embraced her with a cry.

"Oh, God, Celeste, I've been looking for you! Thank God! You're alive! I was right behind you, and you just—you disappeared! I thought you were gone! I thought—Oh thank *God!*"

She fell still, too shocked by the freezing cold to respond.

Celeste lay limp in Theo's hands as he gathered her up and carried her back into the cabin.

CHAPTER TEN

She was feeling warmer now but no better. Describing what she'd seen while submerged in the snow was a challenge. Even when she was in the midst of the story, telling Theo about King Zokkar's hall, his throne, and his dinner guests, she felt she was doing the tale a disservice. The horror of it was simply indescribable without patience, and even though Theo would have sat and listened to her unwind the story detail by detail, she couldn't wait for it to be over. She was already tired of reliving it.

She looked down at the mug of tea Theo had made her. He'd also brought down all the blankets from their bed upstairs, a change of warm clothes, and was periodically hunting for a heating pad he swore his mother sometimes left behind when they visited. He'd also started a fire, which was warming Celeste's back. She sat on the floor, legs crossed, bundled up, trying not to jump when the wood popped and shot sparks behind her.

"Does any of this sound familiar?" Celeste asked.

"I've never dreamed about that city before. I didn't know what happened to Ib, actually. Like I said before, all I knew about it was what I saw in the dreams, and they never went beyond—"

"Sarnath." She took a drink, held it until it was lukewarm, then swallowed. "He called the city Sarnath."

Theo nodded. "They destroyed Ib. They mocked the Old God. The Old God . . . drowned them."

"It sounds like Atlantis."

"It could be." Theo sat down across from her, his back against the coffee table. "It could be that's how the legend began. Then the name got misheard, then mistranslated, then outright changed, then—then on and on and on."

"I had a similar thought after the first dream. The one about Bokrug," Celeste said. "I wondered if the idea of little green Martians came from . . . the Ibians." Her teeth chattered.

Theo slunk toward her and put an arm around her. He started to rub up and down, creating more heat for her to languish in.

"You're going to have a cold," he said.

"But you'll take care of me." She placed her head against his shoulder and closed her eyes.

He pulled her impossibly close. "I promise." His voice cracked.

She was sure he was thinking the same thing she was. Neither of them had been asleep when King Zokkar appeared at the door. They'd been wide awake.

It wasn't a dream ritual anymore, even though it'd

felt like one. It was affecting their waking world. But putting such a terrible thought into words, much less speaking them, was a monumental task Celeste wasn't up to.

She clung tight to Theo, held in her sniffles, and shut her eyes.

"Take me upstairs. I want to go to sleep."

Theo hesitated. "Celeste—"

"It doesn't matter. It's like you said. It'll happen anyways. May as well get it over with."

"I'll stay awake," he said.

"Why?"

"To make sure you don't walk out into the cold again."

She sneezed on cue. "Maybe that's a good idea. But wake me up, yeah? You'll need rest too. Besides, I'm not entirely sure I want to stay on the other side for very long."

He agreed. "Promise me you'll wake up."

"I will." She hoped she wasn't lying.

He scooped her into his arms. It was amazing how weightless she felt when he held her. He walked sideways so she didn't hit her head on the narrow walls beside the stairs. In the bedroom, he laid her down gently, as if worried she'd break.

The moment her head touched the pillow, an unnatural calm claimed her. It swept upon her like a wave, caressing and crushing her simultaneously. She felt flattened and grateful for it.

Today is only Saturday. It feels like we've been here for weeks. Weeks without sleep . . . real sleep . . . restful sleep . . . happy sleep . . .

She tried to talk herself into sleep, and yet it would not come. Celeste pulled the blankets over her head and turned over, hoping a new position would help. When it didn't, she turned back.

"What's this?" Theo asked, rousing her.

"Hmm?" She sat up. "What is it?"

"Oh my God." There was muted panic in his voice.

She saw he was standing by his writing desk. Originally, there'd only been a hardbacked dictionary and a tattered thesaurus, but now Celeste saw a third book had appeared. One she knew hadn't been there before; otherwise, she would have taken interest in it when the Harlan Coben thriller had failed to detach her from her worries.

The book was slender and dusty, with pages as yellow as corn. The binding was worn thin, and the leather cover was coming away in patches. It looked like the book had survived a house flood and then a sun-scorched drought. Whatever color it had been before was so muted, it looked grey now.

She got up to her knees and went to the bed's edge. "What is it?"

He opened the cover, his hands shaking. "I know this book. The last time I saw it . . . I was . . ."

The scampering of padded feet surprised them

both into silence.

"It's the rat again," Celeste said, more to herself than to Theo.

"The what?" he asked.

"Earlier . . . I saw a big rat running around from beneath the bed. I forgot about it until—"

"How big?" Theo demanded.

Unnerved by his tone, she swallowed and answered slowly. "It was big. I don't know exactly. And fast. It probably came in before we did. We always had rats in our house during the winter when I was a kid, so I didn't think too hard about it."

Theo shook his head. "It's not a coincidence. It can't be."

"Can't be *what*?"

A scratching noise came from the walls. It surrounded them, making them both freeze in place and hold their breaths.

"It's been here this whole time. It wasn't Lavinia . . . it wasn't your mother . . . it was *him*."

"Him who?" Celeste asked.

"I never told anyone about it. Even I thought it was insane. Lavinia had . . . a friend is what she called him. He'd be at the rituals with us, just watching from the corner. When we were done, she'd write notes onto little scrolls of paper and hand them to him . . . and he'd carry them away. I asked where he took them, and she always said, 'The Devil.' I didn't believe her. Despite everything she'd shown me and everything she'd done,

I thought it was a rat. Until the day she showed me how she fed it. Until I got a look at his face . . . and heard him talk."

"Theo, who is it?"

"He's called Brown Jenkin," he started.

And then the giant rat came out from below the bed and dashed toward Theo's feet. He scrambled backwards, hitting his rump against the desk. Right when he thought to pull his legs up, the rat bit into his bare heel, cutting its thick teeth into the flesh with a spray of bright blood.

Celeste screamed.

Theo screamed louder.

The rat dangled from his kicking leg, its bulky body flopping back and forth while its head remained latched on vise-tight. Around the flesh and pouring blood, the rat didn't squeak; it garbled.

It sounded like the beast was trying to speak around a mouthful of food.

Theo scrabbled backwards, knocking the books and the fountain pen off the desk. Black ink spread upon the ground, mingling with Theo's blood.

Celeste burst into action. She leapt off the bed, chased after Theo's kicking leg, and then secured her hands around the furry body of the rodent. Touching it was repulsive enough to tickle her gag reflex, but she held it down and dug her fingers in, hoping the creature would release her lover. Still, Theo kicked, pulling Celeste's arms up and down.

The creature squealed, then finally relented. The separation caused Celeste to tip backward and land half on and half off the bed. In a blur, she turned it over in her hands—and screamed anew when she saw its face.

It had the body of a rat, the long, naked, pink tail of a rat, the grungy fur of a rat . . . but there, the similarities ended.

It had hands.

It had hands.

They looked like they belonged to an uncannily accurate doll, with flat fingernails, hairy knuckles, and deep creases in their palms. Baby-like, they clutched at the air between it and her face. She held the beast away from her at arm's length, and even that felt too close for comfort.

It did not have a face. No eyes, no ears, no nose— only an oversized mouth filled with needle-point teeth. Its lips were covered in seeping boils and winking sores.

The creature's repugnant mouth dropped open, and out waggled a raw, swollen, bee-stung tongue.

And then, adding to Celeste's mounting horror . . . it spoke.

Its voice was a guttural, squelching cough.

"Schreibe deinen Namen auf dieses Buch! Deine Spucke ist nicht genug! Wir wollen dein Blut!"

Celeste screamed so loud her vocal cords burned. Her eyes widened, blood vessels popping.

Above her, Theo appeared, his teeth bared. He

grabbed the creature by its thrashing tail. "Let go!" he roared.

She released the monster just as Theo pulled it into the air and *smashed* it into the floor. The tail slipped out of his fist, and the rat rolled away, its humanoid hands clawing at the ground as it tumbled.

Celeste leapt onto the bed. It was her island in a chaotic sea.

The thing came to a stop against the far wall. It lay on the floor, one leg twitching. Its tongue hung from between its teeth, swollen and dripping.

"Did you kill it?" she shrieked.

"I don't think so—"

The creature rolled onto its belly, then pushed itself onto its rear legs. Its clawed hands turned into bundled fists, and its tongue slithered in and out of its crusty maw.

It turned toward Celeste, its mouth stuck in a permanent grin. The monster spoke once again in a voice made out of crunching glass and swallowed phlegm.

"Ich werde an seiner Leiche in der Hölle nagen!" It pointed a crooked finger toward Theo. "Seine Haut wird das Gesicht, das der Teufel verbrannt hat, ersetzen! *Sign the book, whore!*"

Then it fell onto all fours and bounded lopsidedly toward the bedroom door.

"Stop it! Stop it!" Theo shouted, running after the beast.

Celeste was paralyzed. She watched as the creature snaked around the corner and then heard its nails scrabble down the stairs. Theo charged after it, shouting its hideous name.

Brown Jenkin.

A messenger between a witch and the Devil.

She'd seen it earlier. It had been hiding under their bed. Watching them stealthily from the shadows. It'd been a part of their ritual, and it was the reason things had gone haywire. Not her mother, not Lavinia herself, but a demonic servant to the old witch.

Theo came clomping back up the stairs. When he walked into the room, she saw he was empty-handed and crestfallen.

"He . . . slipped away."

She eased herself off the bed. "Where?"

"I almost had him, and then he was just gone."

"Theo . . . what is he?"

He shook his head. "A familiar. He was created a long time ago to serve . . . dark witches." He walked over to the desk and began to pick up the fallen books. There was nothing to be done about the ink spill. It was the least of their collective concerns. When his hands touched the older book, the one that had appeared out of nowhere, he visibly shuddered.

"What's that book, Theo?" she asked. "Why did that . . . *thing* want me to sign it?"

Theo sighed and brought the book to her.

"I know what this all means now, Celeste. I understand what's happening to you."

"Tell me."

He opened the book and handed it to her. She flipped through the pages, baffled by the contents. It seemed like a text book stuffed with Euclidian geometry. Between the shapes, squares, unnatural lines, circles, and starry patterns, there were sketches of strange creatures. Beings that looked like tentacled patches of fungi, creatures with wings draped over their bodies like shrouds, and monsters even uglier than Bokrug. The illustrations began as rudimentary figures, but they became more detailed and fiercer the further into the book she went.

Beside each being was an unpronounceable name.

Yog-Sothoth was a creature with a stalk for a neck, a cone-shaped body, and a beard of tentacles growing from its skull-like face.

Nyarlathotep was an emaciated human body with too-long arms and a writhing, bulging tentacle growing from the space between its shoulders.

The names blurred together, churning in front of her eyes.

Hagarg Ryonis. Ghatanothoa, the firstborn son of the great Cthulhu. Tamash, who dwells in Kadath.

And then she came upon the worst of them all.

It occupied two whole pages, stretching toward their corners as if it wanted to spill out of the pages and come to life in their dark bedroom. A mass of polyps, mouths, tentacles, claws, teeth, and diseased eyes. A floating cloud of wicked matter, composed entirely of pieces too loathsome for even the foulest of his brethren.

Across the pages, written in long-dried blood, was the name *Azathoth*.

She turned the page and found more blood, alongside cursive script.

I doth pledge mine soul and body to the great shepherd of humanity, Azathoth, the King of All Things. Lord of magic and wicked powers. I will sacrifice mine blood unto him, and the blood of others, especially them that kneel at the altar of the falsified messiah, whom I shalt mock and ridicule with mine dark practices, preachery. It is a terrible pilgrimage to seek the nighted throne of the far daemon-sultan Azathoth—whose name is hideous—but it is a pilgrimage I willfully endure to commit mineself to until mine starving days.

Underneath this declaration, four names were etched in blood. Celeste could imagine the haggish women pricking their fingers before sealing their dark commitment to this ancient evil.

Siccician Ullisius

Tartha Inninian

Keziah Mason

Lavinia Whateley

Beside each name was a small handprint, also in blood. Celeste didn't have to guess whose tiny hand had made each mark. She'd seen the rat-beast with her own eyes.

"Lavinia is dying," Theo said, breaking Celeste away from the book with a start. "I don't know how . . . or when . . . but she's dying. And now, she wants you to take her place."

PART THREE

THE DREAM QUEST

"Children will always be afraid of the dark, and men with minds sensitive to hereditary impulse will always tremble at the thought of the hidden and fathomless worlds of strange life which may pulsate in the gulfs beyond the stars, or press hideously upon our own globe in unholy dimensions which only the dead and the moonstruck can glimpse."

H.P. Lovecraft, from his introduction to his essay "Supernatural Horror in Literature."

CHAPTER ELEVEN

It was near midnight now. The hours had drifted away from them, floating like ash flakes caught in a breeze. Celeste waited for an explanation, but Theo was busying himself at the altar they had created out of the coffee table. He reset the candles, relit them, then unwound the bandages around his hand and reopened the wound on his palm.

"What are you doing?" she asked, holding the book at arm's length, wishing she could set it down but also knowing she didn't want the dark thing out of her sight.

Theo didn't answer. He tipped his hand sideways and allowed a sheet of fresh blood to spill into the hungry goblet. He swirled it around, then brought it to her.

"Spit," he said, holding the goblet out.

She shook her head. "Not until you tell me what's going on."

He sighed. "The only reason I've stuck by this ritual is because it was the one that always worked, right?"

"Right."

"That's because *Bokrug* wanted it to work. I prayed to him, and he answered. You prayed to him . . . and you *saw* him."

"Yes. But that was because . . ." She didn't know how to describe it, so she closed her mouth.

"Brown Jenkin wants you to sign your name in Lavinia's book. Lavinia never worshipped Bokrug. Not like I did. Not like you've been doing." Theo narrowed his eyes. "I don't know how to put this, so I'll put it bluntly. She wants you to defy the god you worship and turn to Azathoth. That's what the final part of the ritual is going to become if it goes the way she and Brown Jenkin have scripted it. Do you speak German?"

"No."

"I do. A bit. You know what that *thing* was telling you to do?"

"No! Tell me! I'm tired of all this! Just tell me!" She started to sob again but quickly gained control, pulling her tears back and calming her breath.

"Sorry," Theo muttered, looking toward the goblet he held in his cupped hands. "He said, and this is a rough translation, he wants you to put your name in the book. Under Lavinia's."

Theo paced suddenly away from her, toward the glass door. He slid it open and tossed the contents of the goblet into the snow, then slammed it shut. In the miniscule amount of time the door had been open, gooseflesh had broken out like an infection down the lengths of Celeste's limbs.

"We're taking too long. It wouldn't work," Theo explained. "You know how witches are made, Celeste? Not the witches in movies but the ones in real life, with real power?"

She shook her head. Of course she didn't, and she hated that he was still asking questions as if to gauge whether or not she believed in what was happening to her.

"A witch has to do more than study dark magic and write letters to the Devil. A witch has to see God . . . and then deny Him. Everything they do is an act of . . . of spiritual mockery. They get power from cosmic anger."

"So, she's been, what, setting up meetings between me and Bokrug, just so I'll turn my back on him?"

"Exactly!" Theo nodded. "And then, when you do, when you put your blood on the pages of their book, she'll transfer everything she has to you. All her knowledge. All her power. All her twisted, fucked-up ideas. All her wickedness. All her . . . familiars."

"You mean there's more?"

"Lord knows how many. Brown Jenkin is always their favorite, but every witch has a horde of imps that keep them company."

"You've seen all of this?"

Theo nodded again. "Up close."

"When you were a child, was this the sort of stuff she—"

"It's why I don't talk about it. If I did, I'd get sent away again." Theo suppressed a sudden flare of red in his cheeks. "When I told my parents, I didn't just tell them about the rituals, about the abuse. I also told them Lavinia could talk to shadows, and rats with human mouths, and demons with forked tongues and curly tails and pitch forks and—and they sent me to a doctor, who convinced me I'd come up with a fantasy about 'Hell' to cope with having something I didn't understand happen to me. He said it was natural. A lot of traumatized kids make up fantasies to rationalize things that scared them. He told me I didn't need to worry about being dragged to Hell by demons. But that didn't stop me from waking up screaming every night for a year straight. That didn't stop the bad dreams from coming back when I least expected them." He shivered. "I . . . I think she was grooming me to take her place. And because I broke our pact, she's taking you now, just to spite me. Just to rub it in my face that she can take whatever she wants from me. Just to punish me for—" Theo wiped away a tear, leaving a bloody streak on his cheek. "Just to punish me for having moved on from her. For finding you. For falling in love. For being happy."

Celeste started toward him, sympathetic and calm.

"But I'm not going to let her!" Theo burst out, his fury startling. He turned away and set the goblet back on the coffee table. Again, he picked up his curvy blade and scraped it across his palm. Blood welled up around the edge of the knife, staining its shimmery surface.

"Lavinia took a lot from me. I won't let her take you. There's no way we can stop the ritual, but now that we know what it is . . . maybe we can *change* it."

Celeste came to his side and gripped his arm with her hand, holding the book to her chest all the while.

"What do you need?"

He held the goblet up. "Spit first. Then, I'm afraid you're going to have to bleed."

Celeste nodded, tilted her head down, and produced a white spittle. It dripped lightly into the bloody goblet.

He set the goblet down in the middle of the candle-lit circle, then placed the blade in her open palm. "I'm sorry, you have to do it yourself."

She moved toward the table, but Theo caught her by the wrist.

"I haven't done a great job preparing you for these things. I don't know exactly what will happen next, Celeste, but it will be a lot."

She grimaced. "I think I already know it'll be worse if I don't."

"What we're doing . . . it will change you. You won't come out of this as the person you are right now. Not entirely. If this works, you'll come back a different kind of witch than the one Lavinia wants you to be . . . but you'll be a witch all the same."

She didn't know how to take that.

"What we're doing is setting up our own meeting with Bokrug. This time, you're going to pledge yourself to him. That's a pledge you can't break. It's something you'll have to keep until you die. And it means when that day comes . . . you won't go to Heaven. You won't go to Hell. You'll go . . . to him."

She saw, behind her blinking lids, the smoggy substance rising from Bokrug's terrible mouth, swirling with faces caught in permanent screams.

Bokrug or Azathoth . . . her choices both led toward misery.

But at least one would be at her own volition, not the whims of a hag who she only knew by name. It was, at least for the moment, the sort of illusionary independence she required to make her decision.

"It's him or her, isn't it?" she asked.

"I'm afraid so. I'm sorry, Celeste. I really am. I never wanted this."

"I believe you."

The ground started to shake beneath them. Theo held his arms out to keep his balance. The candles flickered but were not extinguished. The blood inside the goblet trembled.

"Hurry, Celeste! They'll be coming to stop this! They can tell what we're doing!"

She closed her eyes and fell to her knees beside the table. From behind, she heard glass shatter. It was like a poltergeist attack. Some invisible force pulled cups, bowls, plates, and pans out of the cupboards and smashed them onto the kitchen floor. From upstairs, she heard the window shatter, snow blowing into the house in a temperamental rush. The bedsheets ripped apart like paper. The tearing sounds were like squeals from a slaughterhouse.

The wind increased, blasting the house like it wanted to tear the four walls down and dig through its contents. Celeste didn't have to struggle to picture immense claws falling from the sky and scraping the earth open in search of her and her lover.

She set the book on the ground. It flipped over and broke open, the pages spinning like a rolodex before landing on the full portrait of Azathoth, Lavinia's favorite of the Old Gods. The illustration looked even more realistic and frightful than before. The tendrils and rotten-skinned limbs appeared to break out of the pages and lash toward her, but only in strobe-lit bursts. One second, it was a 2D image, the next, it was pulsating with viscid life, and then it was back to a crude drawing, caught and bound by the split between the pages. A pool of slimy shadows expanded beneath the book, spreading on the floor.

The fireplace coughed sparks. Instantly, a curtain caught. Orange tiptoes walked toward the wall.

Theo leapt into action, grabbing the curtains and yanking them off the rod. They smoldered on the floor while he stomped on them, compressing the flames into the ground.

Celeste laid the blade on her right palm. She sealed her hand into a tight fist around it. Already, the curved edges bit into her flesh. It stung like a hornet, flushing her skin and prickling the hairs on her arm.

Okay, Bokrug . . . I accept that I believe in you. I saw how terrible you are, how cruel. But I'm the only person on Earth that knows your name.

You smite me, you smite yourself!

So let's talk. Let's actually talk, you and I. Maybe we can come to an understanding.

The floorboards rattled as if a train was passing the cabin. Behind her closed eyes, she saw a light sway back and forth, making her seasick. Then she heard a bulb break. Then another.

The earthquake stilled, stopping so suddenly it almost spilled her onto the floor. Her guts shifted uneasily, and she sucked in a breath and held it like she expected to be doused in cold water.

Darkness claimed her, sealing her vision behind tight hands when she opened her eyes. All she could see was the pale, ghostly glow of the snow reflecting what little of the moon peered through the storm.

"Theo?" she asked.

"Celeste?" His voice was far away. It echoed as if he was shouting to her from the end of a very long tunnel. *Or from the back of a crypt*, she thought with a quiver.

She held her hand toward the circle of snuffed candles. The more her eyes adjusted, the more she saw. Sheaths of smoke floated around the candles' heads. Wax bulged down their shafts, wet and sleek.

She felt her blood patter on the table's surface. She was near the goblet now but hadn't landed a drop.

Celeste heard feet racing behind her. Something big was coming.

She turned her head.

"Theo?" she asked, hoping the shadows would

break and her boyfriend would appear.

The footsteps came closer, each one striking like a hammer on moist wood. The house creaked and groaned as the being approached, each footstep causing it to jarringly shake.

The approaching figure loomed, cast in thick, cloying shadows. It looked like a clot detaching itself from a polyp. Then, as it neared, it took concrete shape, growing taller, thinner, and firmer.

It's coming . . .

It had a white face, blurred like a shaky photograph. Its skull was as round as a cue ball, and it had soft, wet eyes, which were like train lights at the end of dark tunnels.

It's coming . . .

It stomped toward her, each footstep longer than the last. It walked uncannily, as if it was trying to sneak but was also failing to be quiet on purpose. Its arms lurched toward her, each motion a swipe in the air. Its fingers were flat as paper.

It's coming . . .

And then it started to take a real shape. It blurred further, becoming an animated smudge. Then it stiffened . . . and out of the darkness, it charged, making up the space between the wall of shadows and the small circle of lighter darkness that had become Celeste's immediate field of vision.

It's here . . .

The mother-thing that had last haunted her in the

upstairs bedroom streamed out of the shadows. Not a ghost, as she'd first assumed, but an alien shapeshifter. A cosmic entity that worked, like Brown Jenkin, for Lavinia Whateley. A thing that's true image was imageless, but who had the awesome and terrible ability to steal the form of another's worst nightmares.

Stealthy and militaristic, the thing which looked like a long-limbed, blind-eyed version of Celeste's mother leapt toward her, arms outreached, mouth agape and filled with razor-sharp teeth.

Without moving its unhinged mouth, it released an airy rasp. It was a scream without vocal cords. Dry and rattling, the loathsome noise made Celeste's ears ring.

The creature's fangs flashed toward her. In seconds, they would be upon her. They would tear the flesh from her skull in one bite, leaving her crumpled and agonized on the ground. They'd make Theo freeze to death, abandoned in the cabin, waiting for her to come back from the pitch-dark netherworld they'd cornered her in.

It'd rather have killed myself, she thought as she held in a scream and waited for the inevitable assault of teeth and claws.

A drop of Celeste's blood fell from between her knuckles and *plinked* into the goblet like a coin in a fountain.

There was a sudden gasp of breath, and then the mother-thing was gone.

So, too, was Celeste's eyesight.

She stood stiff, holding out her bloody hand beside

her. Small ropes of blood did loop-the-loops as they fell away from her and slapped onto the flat ground where the coffee table had once sat.

Waiting for her eyes to readjust proved fruitless. This was darker than the shadow-place she'd just come from. This was true-darkness. The last time she'd experienced it, she'd been sealed within the mouth of an ancient god, certain she had already been consumed.

Bokrug . . .

Chapter Twelve

At least she had control of her feet. She couldn't see where she was going, but she walked on anyways, pushing her hands ahead of her, one sticky with blood and the other bare. The dagger had slipped out of her grasp in the eye-blink between one world and the next. She wished she had it still so she wouldn't feel totally defenseless. Not that a dagger (no matter how magical) could do much against ancient gods and alien monsters.

Celeste hoped her hands would act as a subconscious divining rod, leading her where she needed to be. She tried to step forward, but it was like walking on air. The sensation unnerved her, making her feel as if she was taking a step off the edge of a sheer cliff.

She tested her mouth, speaking into the unventilated nothingness that confined her. She couldn't hear the sound of her own voice. Nothing came out of her. Not even breath. She knew if she was on Earth, in the real world, she'd be suffocating. But she didn't need to breathe anymore, just as she didn't need to see.

She plunged forward, into the darkness, finally acclimating to the new environment. Her hands, stretched ahead of her, felt nothing. It was as if she was walking in a sensory deprivation tank. No sound, no smell, no touch . . . nothing.

Nothing.

Nothing.

The nothingness a god dwells in when people cease to worship him. The nothingness God Himself experienced before he said, "Let there be light." The nothingness all humans know before they rest in the womb. The nothingness beyond life, death, and other such miniscule concepts.

There was no temperature. No hot or cold.

Then there came a voice. Far away and clipped, it sent out scattered words in a dark tone. She recognized it as Brown Jenkin, the evil witch's shadowy familiar. Shuddering at the memory of the ratlike demon, she pushed ahead, even though the voice grew in cadence and volume as she walked. Soon, it was upon her, speaking in French. Before, she'd had no clue what Brown Jenkin had said to her, but Celeste had studied French on-and-off when she was a student, and even though it had been some time since she last practiced, she was versed enough to get the gist of what Brown Jenkin was demanding of her.

"Après que tu auras inscrit ton nom dans notre livre noir, sorcière, je téterai ton doigt ensanglanté!"

After you've signed your name in our black book, witch, I will suckle from your bleeding finger!

A gruesome vignette appeared behind the obscuring darkness. She saw herself in Lavinia's place, haggard and frayed, worn down by the darkness she consumed. She envisioned herself scratching out a wicked message on a tiny piece of parchment and rolling it into a little scroll, bound with hairy twine. Then she saw herself prick her finger to feed the grunting rat that sat upon her desk. After he nursed, he'd take her message to the Devil. To Azathoth. And whatever she wrote would be, no matter how abhorrent, made true. The way it had been for Lavinia.

She attempted to speak again and was surprised when her voice leaked out between her bared teeth.

"My blood is sacred. I offer it only to the Oldest God." She hadn't planned it out, but she spoke as if she was reading from a script.

"Mets fin à tes jours si tu ne veux plus rêver de nous!" Brown Jenkin responded, his voice larger than his body had been.

"You first," Celeste grunted. She pushed forward, incapable of running but desperate to. She could hear Jenkin's wheezing breath as the creature scampered away from her as if dodging her footsteps.

You better run. I've seen my god, Brown Jenkin. He's bigger than yours.

She couldn't know whether that was true or not. What if Azathoth made Bokrug look miniscule in comparison?

She needed faith, not doubt. She pictured an image of the Great Water Lizard and was awed once again by his size. The creature she'd seen in her first vision of the weekend had been large (and terrible) enough to swallow the moon with ease.

IÄ . . . IÄ . . . Bokrug . . .

A simple prayer. It spun out of her like thread.

IÄ . . . IÄ . . . Bokrug . . .

The darkness broke. Ahead of her, a pale-green mist fell from the heavens and enveloped a humanoid shape. It was formless and sexless, simply a silhouette with arms and legs and a tall, noble head.

Celeste could breathe again. The air was acrid and tart. It sizzled her tongue and burned all the way down her throat. Her lungs were engulfed, and her blood simmered.

She walked toward the misty figure, but every step she took seemed to push the thing away from her. It was like the watery haze that grew ahead of a car on a hot highway.

"Who are you?" she asked.

There came no reply. The green figure continued to slink just out of reach. It remained a still image, and yet it moved, taking the mist with it.

IÄ . . . IÄ . . . Bokrug . . .

The figure stood still, allowing her a few more steps before it shifted out of reach once more.

Celeste swallowed thickly, wishing Theo was here to guide her. Maybe this was part of some obscure ritual he'd read about before and could offer guidance toward completing. At the same time, she knew he was facing horrors of his own, trapped in the house with Lavinia's familiars. The shapeshifter, Brown Jenkin, and who knew what else.

"Please . . . wait for me!" Celeste broke into a sprint. Her muscles crinkled like she'd just awoken from a coma. "Wait!"

She was running now, and the ghostly specter continued to evade her.

"Wait!" Celeste screamed. "Wait for me!"

She pumped her arms and legs, but it felt like running on a treadmill. Sweat glossed her skin (her clothing hadn't come to this alternate dimension with her). Was this some sort of cosmic joke? she wondered. Had they brought her here just to chase a will-o-the-wisp for eternity, ashamed and naked?

"Please," she whimpered.

IÄ . . . IÄ . . . Bokrug . . .

The moment she thought the chant, which she'd first heard roared by an ancient civilization from before man, from before history, the green figure stilled. It was jarring, the way the creature stopped. Almost as if it had phased from a gas to a solid in a photo-flash. Then it was moving again, just out of reach.

It's him.

It's what's left of him.

What's actually left of him.

Not an ancient God floating in a tank of dark matter but a memory of a memory of a memory. A memory that remembers itself, that can project what it once was . . . but is, in truth, in flesh, in actuality, nothing more than a scrap left over from a world that's been buried and forgotten.

This is Bokrug.

He needs your strength, Celeste.

He needs your prayers.

Celeste tried to clear her mind. It was a near impossible task. Every second, she was bombarded with new worries and confusions. And after so long without proper sleep, her brain was deluded. It wandered around the facts and the nightmares, connecting the two with thin strips of Scotch tape. She tried to close her eyes, but the darkness behind her lids did nothing to calm her.

It's not about being calm. It's about being passionate. It's about believing.

Bokrug wants your belief. It's valuable. It's coveted.

Give him a sample.

Celeste spoke in her sternest, most sincere voice, not believing the words herself until they'd broken out of her.

"*IÄ . . . IÄ . . . Bokrug!*"

The green figure stilled again.

"*IÄ! IÄ!*" Celeste declared, clenching her hands into fists and skidding to a stop. "*IÄ!*"

The figure stood ahead of her, head slightly cocked, arms flat by its sides. The green mist congregated around the spirit, shimmering like a mistreated bridal veil over his distorted features.

"No!" Celeste barked. "I'm not coming to you! If you want my faith . . . *you come to me!*" She took a step backward.

The green mist began to waver. She saw solid matter behind it. Patches of diseased and flaking scales. Briefly, a clawed hand swiped through the clouds, parting them. She heard something rumble in the distance, like an insulted volcano.

"That's the way it's going to be," Celeste said below her breath. "If you want to be worshipped, you have to earn it. I've had enough of your rituals. I'm making my own."

She took another step back.

A raspy shriek rose from the figure. It seemed to tilt on its side, one arm jutting out of the fog, the other welded to its body.

"I'll pray to you. I'll make converts of others. I'll write my name in blood upon the pages of a new book . . . one we'll write together. I'll bury Azathoth and Yog-Sothoth and Cthulhu and all your selfish brothers who *stole* from you. I'll be the best witch you've ever had, Bokrug. But I will not worship you for free."

The ground shook beneath her, drawing her thoughts back to the cabin, to the spiritual temper tantrum ripping through the kitchen, shattering plates and glasses.

"Ythhuga torh kath daggatar!" the creature roared.

Celeste took another step back. "I'll go back. I'll

go all the way back. And when I die . . . when they kill what's left of me and replace my insides with Azathoth's will . . . no one will ever be afraid of *you* ever again. No one." Celeste showed her teeth. "Do you understand what that means?"

"Ythhuga—*You will do well to fear me, child—*torh kath—*I smote Sarnath and I shall smite you—*daggatar—*The Old Ones are incapable of Death. It eludes us. You cannot threaten me, girl. You cannot scare me into submission!*"

"You may never die. But you'll never be powerful. You'll be stuck here . . . forever."

"*I'll live on in dreams and nightmares. In unknown corners of maddened minds. You'll never be rid of me—*"

"Nightmares are easy to forget. Even yours." Celeste stepped backward again.

The green figure lurched toward her, arms outstretched. She only saw a flash of its inhuman face. Fishlike, with multiple tongues hanging heavily from its drooping jaws. The creature snapped backward, obscured once more by the mist.

"You can't even startle me," Celeste affirmed, straightening her back and lifting her chin.

The beast spoke in thunder.

"*I am older even than you know.*"

She took a step toward him. Her tone now was gentle and understanding. "And you have many stories to tell. Many commandments to make. Many gods to devour . . ."

The creature shrank back from her. "*I do not need humanity.*"

"No. Of course not. You could live here forever, couldn't you? Long after humanity has been replaced and forgotten. But why would you *want to*? Why would you rather sleep . . . when you could inspire . . . and terrify?" She took another step closer to the shrouded creature. "Azathoth wants me. But I'm willing to give myself to you."

Bokrug said nothing. Instead, his glowing eyes (she couldn't count how many there were) gazed at her through the mist, each shining now like a flashlight. She was enraptured by their brilliance, but not enough to lose focus of what she knew needed done. She froze in place, refusing to take the next step, the one that would put her within Bokrug's green smog.

"We'll never be equals, Bokrug," Celeste said. "But you need me, and I can give you what you need . . . so long as you reward me."

"*How?*" Bokrug croaked.

"I will write your Bible. I will worship you. I will serve you. In exchange . . ." She fell to her knees, not even flinching when they struck the solid ground. She clasped her hands desperately together and held them out ahead of her. "I want power. I want familiars. I want what Lavinia has. I want to do your will, and I want to do my own."

Bokrug snorted. "*Power? And what would you do with it?*"

Celeste blinked away a tear. "I want to keep what

I have. I don't want wealth. I don't want dominance. I want . . . happiness. And the only way I can have that is by giving you my soul. So I will. I'll give it gladly."

Bokrug stepped toward her. There was a fetid heat that clung to the quilt of fog surrounding him. It was the last of his worshipers who'd given themselves to him, devoured and drained over all these centuries. She could see skinny faces hanging in the mist, caught mid-scream.

"*I will ask terrible things of you,*" Bokrug said. "*Sacrifices must be made.*"

Celeste braced herself. "I would rather make them for you than for the Devil."

Bokrug released a susurrating gurgle. Another step brought him toward Celeste. "*Azathoth has worshipers aside from Lavinia. They must be found and destroyed. Are you up for such . . . tasks?*"

She nodded. If they were even half as cruel as Lavinia, she didn't imagine she'd have many qualms over killing them.

"As long as I can keep what I have."

"*The selfless thing would be to kill yourself.*" Bokrug sneered. She saw his yellowed teeth cutting into his swollen tongues. He was speaking without using his mouth, speaking directly in her head. "*If you did . . . neither Lavinia nor I would be able to claim you. You'd escape all of this.*"

Celeste understood. "But I'd be leaving too much behind. I'm not willing to do that."

"*Why?*"

"Because enough has been taken from me." She shifted. "I'm only just now starting to feel alive."

"*Because of love?*"

"In a way."

"*Theo will not stay with you when he sees what you are becoming. When he sees what you . . . are capable of.*" Bokrug snickered.

"It isn't about him." A defiant tear streaked down her cheek. "And it is. I want him, but I won't force him to stay if he doesn't want to. But it's about more than him."

Celeste lowered her head. It was impossible to stop the weeping now. She eked her words out between sobs.

"I . . . want . . . to . . . *be.*"

She felt Bokrug's clawed hand touched the back of her head. It was at once soothing and repulsive.

"*Be . . . what?*"

"I just want to be." As simple as it was, that was the root of all this. She wanted to be herself when she was all alone in her home, she wanted to be herself when she was with Theo, she'd wanted to be herself when she was growing up. And every time she'd tried, there'd been an obstacle. Something stuck in her way or some force beyond her control. Something that compressed her and demanded servility and compliance from her. Something like Lavinia, who had machinations in mind for her despite her own wants and desires.

It all felt like it had led to this. To the meeting between her and Bokrug. To two beings demanding worship of each other in different voices. If she did what Bokrug wanted, then he would return the favor. And what she wanted was for her own self to simply exist. And that . . . that would be enough.

"*Then . . . we have much in common,*" Bokrug said.

He lifted his claw from her.

She held up her head.

Celeste was kneeling on the edge of a cliff. Underneath her, she could hear the ocean.

She tried to pull her clasped hands apart. They were bound.

A cloth had been tied around her skull, blinding one eye and drooping down so the left could see. The fabric irritated the eye, meaning she could only see in brief flashes, opening and shutting her eye rapidly so that the world strobed around her.

She wore nothing otherwise.

Below her, there were empty caves. She could hear the wind screaming through their tunnels. If there'd been worshipers, they would have been chanting Bokrug's name. All she could hear was the screeching wind, the crashing ocean waves, and her own thumping heartbeat.

Hollow like an abandoned wasp's nest, the sheer cliff that had once been Ib was, like Bokrug, a ghost of its former self. How often, she wondered, did she drink water that was filled with fossilized ghosts? How often did she breathe the same air that had been sucked into the lungs of Ibians and Sarnathians? She was certain there was eternal life now (more than she'd ever been when her mother preached of Heaven and Hell), but it was a dismal thing, eternity. It was a silent scream trapped within the fabric of an atom. It was lurking within the shadows beneath blades of grass, watching distantly as the world expanded and mutated and evolved beyond recognition.

And I, too, will experience this. I will know all Bokrug knows. I'll even, someday, forget my own name. Will it be worth it? Will giving up my soul be worth it in a century? In a thousand centuries?

She thought of Theo. He'd been so harmed by the terrors she was now hurtling toward. He'd been wounded by a woman who'd mistreated him, all for her own personal gain. He had never intended for Celeste to face the same horrors he had, and yet he'd guided her here just the same. She could only hope he would remain by her side the way she wanted to be by his. That even as her powers became overwhelming, he would remain her guiding light. That he would love her the way she needed to be loved.

I will not do what Lavinia did. Ever. But I will remind him of her nonetheless, simply for being powerful, for worshipping these ancient gods, for reminding him of the parts of himself he's too fascinated by to abandon. We will never grow or change. We'll stay the same. And that alone will be its own challenge.

Is this selfish? Should I have killed myself?

No. It's the only choice. If I'd killed myself, I would

*have given them my life anyways. At least this way . . .
I can take something back.*

It was a struggle to stand with her hands cinched so tightly together, but she made it up to her wobbling feet and inched closer to the edge.

I will worship you, Bokrug. Only you. Even in my screaming moments before death, I will think only of you.

She held her hands above her head, striking a pose she'd seen only once before.

She could feel him behind her, too impatient to remain hidden. He'd grown bigger in the moments since she last saw him. His bulk towered above her. She could feel multiple tongues lashing toward her, hovering around her body but not touching it.

She leaned backwards and felt the heaviness of his snout, the heat of his breath. She inhaled, languishing in the rotted odor he carried with him. It was a smell that burned the surface of her face.

"I will serve you," she declared.

"Only me." His voice was firmer than before. Louder.

"Only you."

She fell forward.

C H A P T E R   T H I R T E E N

The idol came crashing down upon Brown Jenkin's body.

Celeste was shocked awake. With a roar of panic, she ripped herself away from the idol. It'd been glued to her hands, and a layer of skin came away from her palms, filling her eyes with white heat.

"It's over!" she heard Theo shout behind her.

Celeste landed on her rump and screamed again. It felt as if she'd been shot from one scene to another from a catapult. She hurriedly looked around, taking in what she could.

The interior of the cabin had been ruined. Holes were punched through the walls, allowing sunlight and snow to stream in. The screen door had been torn, and the sliding glass was shattered. Behind her, the fireplace had been gutted, as if a monstrous Santa had fought his way out of it. All that remained of the coffee table, which had become their ritual altar, was splintered wood. Dogs had attacked the furniture, every window was either spider-webbed or vacant, and the ground was coated in a glossy layer of glass and snow. The two melded together, each a crystalline powder.

And ahead of her, there stood an erect idol. Three feet tall and built of solid stone, it was Bokrug. Reptilian, multi-tongued, multi-eyed, crowned with jewels.

Theo knelt beside her, holding her shoulders.

"Celeste? Are you awake? Are you—are you here?"

"What happened?" she demanded.

"You disappeared." He took her into his arms and squeezed her tight. She was thankful for the contact. The last thing that had touched her had been Bokrug, and it had been foul. She clutched him close, burying her cheek into his chest but keeping her face toward the idol.

Bokrug had stamped Brown Jenkin into a puddle. The raw tail and a single human hand stuck out beneath it, each weakly risen from a pool of quickly congealing blood.

"Where'd you go?" Theo asked.

She ignored the question. Celeste wasn't ready to answer it. "What happened? How'd I . . ."

"You came out of nowhere. Just as Brown Jenkin was about to kill me . . . you came running out of the snow and through the door." He pointed.

"I did that?"

"You came right through the glass. Then you started to beat him to death with . . . with that. The other familiar, the shapeshifter, ran away screaming. I've never seen a frightened demon before, but—" He didn't seem to know what else there was to say. Celeste was glad of it. She could only picture how crazed she looked in the moment, and she was glad she'd never know *exactly* what it had been like. As far as she'd known, she'd been just about to fall off the cliff and into the ancient ocean—and then she'd come awake when the deed was done, when Brown Jenkin was dealt with.

Celeste crawled out of Theo's arms and toward the idol. She took it by its sides and lifted it. There was barely anything left of Lavinia's favorite familiar underneath. She'd beaten him more than the once. Had flattened him to a paste. Chips of rotten teeth floated in the greasy patch of gore.

She let the idol fall back into place. It was heavier than a cinder block. She couldn't imagine *running* with it, much less pounding a rat-demon to death with it.

Celeste turned back to Theo. "I went to Bokrug."

Theo nodded. "Did you . . . ?"

"I think I did whatever his equivalent of 'signing the book' is."

Theo's face crumbled. "We can figure it out later. We just . . . can't stay here. Lavinia is still out there and—"

"I don't think we have to run," Celeste said. Her voice was calmer than even she expected.

"Why not? One of her familiars is still nearby. If she tells it to, it can—"

Celeste stood and walked purposefully toward the broken table. She went to her knees and picked through the rubble, casting aside snuffed candles and Theo's black bag.

"What are you looking for?" he asked.

"The book."

"It's . . . it's upstairs. After you vanished, there was some time before they came back. I brought it back upstairs. I thought maybe if I could fall asleep, I could follow you. Then the familiars came back." He left the rest unspoken.

Celeste stood, went toward him, and kissed him. It was brief.

"Start the car, Theo," she said.

"What are you going to do? You're not going to—"

"I'm not signing it, and I'll explain later. Just . . . heat up the car. And wait for me, okay? Just wait for me."

He shook his head. "I don't want to leave you alone."

"You aren't." She squeezed his hand. "Just let me take care of this. When I'm done, the only thing we'll have left to fear is ourselves."

This sent another wave of confusion through him, but he couldn't disobey her. She knew how she sounded. Resolved. Affirmed. In charge. She sounded, for the first time, like she knew more about Magick and Old Gods than he did. That it wasn't his world anymore

. . . it was theirs.

He peeled away from her. Before she could turn away, he grabbed her wrist and lifted her hand. "You're hurt."

"I think my hands froze against the stone when I was outside." *A reminder from Bokrug that I'm a witch now but that doesn't make me invulnerable. As if I needed one.*

"When you're done . . . I'll take care of this." He was careful to rub his thumb against the back of her hand rather than the sore palm. "I'll take care of you."

She smiled. "I know you will. But let me take care of you first, okay?"

He showed her his own raw palm. "You already did."

They kissed again. This time, they held each other as if there was no urgency left to spare. As if the world had stopped turning. As if Bokrug and Azathoth and Lavinia could wait. When they finally pulled apart, their lips stuck together for a brief moment, chilled together.

"Go," she said. "I'm right behind you."

Theo left.

The cabin was empty.

C HAPTER F OURTEEN

Celeste went up the stairs. It felt like she was crawling up to the cliff's edge once again. Only this time, she was certain she wouldn't fall.

Long claw marks were left on either side of the stairway, torn into the wooden paneling. A bloody handprint lay on every individual step, each the size of a thumb pad. The familiars had torn after Theo, destroying everything that came their way as they hunted him through his own cabin.

She stepped into the bedroom, having to walk over the battered door that lay in three pieces on the floor. The bed had been shredded. Stuffing and springs went in all directions. The blankets had been turned into pom-poms.

The closet was a disaster. Celeste knew none of her possessions could be reclaimed from this weekend. She was lucky enough to be leaving with her life.

Ink, paper, and chunks of broken wood were dispersed around the writing desk, but the book atop it had been left unmolested. It was firmly closed.

She opened it, flipping once more through its

pages and observing the etchings within. The Euclidian horrors, the cosmic deities, the ancient monsters . . . they looked like cartoon characters to her now. No more terrifying than an alien creature from a low-budget shlock flick.

She shut the book and lay a bloody hand upon it.

"*Lavinia*," she said, speaking from her mouth and mind at once. "*I can feel your blood. Dried upon these pages. You are here. You are here. You are here with me.*"

The wind began to scream. It ran into the house like flooding water. Catlike, it crept up the stairs, following in her footsteps. The chill didn't bother her. Instead, she felt herself comforted by it.

If I'm a witch, then I'll be an icy one, she thought. *I'll be Winter's Great Mistress. The Queen of Snow and Howling Wind. What is winter if not an extension of the sea? Of endlessness and of freezing death? Come to me, Lavinia. If you want power . . . I'll show it to you.*

She opened the book and turned the pages until she came upon the list of witch names. She closed her hand into a fist, digging her nails into her naked palm. More blood came from her, filling the bowl of her hand.

She lifted her hand toward her mouth and drank, sipping the blood as if she was a fawn at a sheltered brook. The blood (tangy and harsh) swept down her throat and filled her belly.

After drinking, she turned and went to the hollowed mattress. On its surface, she let her blood dribble into a circle, and then she cut a jagged line through it. The symbol of doom. The Doom that had come to Sarnath and now the Doom that came to Lavinia.

The Doom that was Celeste's to fear and love.

The Doom that was Bokrug.

"Messias et ellitian . . ." She didn't know what the words meant until they were spoken. "IÄ, Bokrug, IÄ."

She shook her hands, spattering blood across the mattress, the torn sheets, the feathers that wafted around in the wind from tattered pillows.

She turned away and hid her eyes with her bloody hands, smearing her face.

"Bring to me Lavinia. Bring her to me so I can kill her."

She turned and looked back at the mattress.

Lavinia lay on the bed behind her, conjured from wherever she'd been hiding. The old woman was too decrepit to be surprised. She lay on her back, crumpled into the soggy, tattered mess that had once been a mattress. She looked like a rat in a nest of stripped sheets and pillow stuffing, her face painted with distressed shock.

"*Azathoth!*" the witch brayed, pointing a crooked finger at Celeste. "*Azathoth! Kill her! Kill this bitch!*"

The woman was skeletal, with wispy strands of white hair hanging in clumps off her papery scalp. One eye was milk white, and the other was yellowed. Her mouth hung open in shock, exposing toothless, black gums. She wore nothing but a sack-cloth, like a deranged peasant from medieval days. Her throat was bulbous with goiters, and each nail was a yellow woodchip. If Lavinia was capable of standing and fighting, she could have clawed Celeste's flesh to ribbons with those claws. Unfortunately for the older witch, her fingers were knotted and arthritic, twisted like overgrown roots beneath a dry shrub.

Celeste stepped toward the bed's edge. "Hail Bokrug," she intoned.

"How . . . dare . . ." Lavinia croaked. "Azathoth . . . will . . . make . . ."

"For what you did to Theo, for what you tried to do to me . . . I'm going to kill you," Celeste stated. Her voice was gentler than she'd anticipated. It did not waver.

Lavinia snarled. Her nostrils were so mucus-caked they cracked like knuckles when they flared. She held her hands up and flexed her fingers. Small sparks flew from between them, as if her nails were made of steel.

"I can shred the skin from your bones, child! My Brown Jenkin and I will make garlands from your innards and—"

"Speak again and suffer."

"Azathoth—" Lavinia tilted her head back and cried out. One of her clawed hands went for her throat.

Celeste grinned, showing all her teeth to the witch. "Now . . . *listen.*"

Lavinia's muddled eyes seeped tears. Her mouth jabbered, but no sound came forth. She tried to squirm away from Celeste, toward the corner of the bed, but there was little she could do. She was trapped within the confines of the bloody circle Celeste had drawn.

Celeste put her bleeding hands on Lavinia's ankles and gripped them tightly. The flesh rasped beneath her hands.

"I'm leaving you here. It's where you belong. You'll starve . . . you'll grow weary . . . and then you'll die. And you'll die having displeased your god. What, Lavinia, do you think he'll do to you when you're with him? Will you be rewarded?"

Lavinia's mouth flapped. Her yellow eye pleaded.

"Your ritual wasn't strong enough. *Mine is.* And my ritual will keep you in this circle, in the cold. You're doomed, Lavinia. *Doomed.* Just as you wanted to doom Theo and me." She released Lavinia's ankles and stepped back. "I'm free to leave. After all of this . . . I'm free. You? You'll just have to lie here and rot." She picked up the book off the desk and showed it to the witch, whose single working eye grew wider with panic. "And this . . . this will burn."

"N-no . . ." Lavinia groaned. The single word brought her instant and obvious pain.

"Starve and suffer." Celeste started toward the door.

Lavinia's hand lashed out and ensnared her arm. There was no violence, only desperation.

"Please . . . just . . . kill . . . me . . ." Lavinia said. "I . . . will . . . take . . . a long . . . time . . . to—" She was suddenly overwhelmed with tormented coughs.

The witch drew her arm back and cradled it, curling in on herself in her magic circle. Weak and pathetic, she whimpered. Her tears froze as they left her eyes.

"This is what you've earned. Enjoy it," Celeste said.

"Please . . . please . . ." Lavinia groaned. "*Please!*"

Celeste went out the bedroom and down the steps.

She expected to hear one last cry from Lavinia, but the witch was in too much pain. Celeste had put barbed needles in her throat, each one perpetually hot and twisting. In the living room, the Bokrug statue stood above its defeated foe. Brown Jenkin's blood had frozen on the ground, turning a shade of crimson so dark it was nearly black.

Bokrug's multiple eyes were sightless, and yet she met them. Hunkering down in front of the statue, she smeared a bloodstained hand across his snout, dousing it in red.

"Whatever you want . . . ask," she said, her voice as dry as a creaking bough. "Whatever you want."

She didn't believe she was outside until the snow was ankle deep and the wind was caressing her face. Again, it didn't freeze her. Gone was the pain she'd experienced in her first frightening dream, the one that had first introduced her to Bokrug. She looked at her palms and saw Theo would have an easy job ahead of him when they finally got home.

Her wounds were already healing.

C HAPTER   F IFTEEN

The lovers drove down the mountain, back the way they'd come. Time meant nothing to either of them. The drive was both a race and a plod, curving down the steep mountain and back toward Salt Lake City.

"You'll tell me everything you did, won't you?" Theo asked.

He'd been confused when she'd told him they needed to build a fire before they left. They'd had to start it with gasoline, pouring it on the open book before lighting it ablaze. When there was nothing left of Azathoth's bible but ash, then they'd climbed into the car and left the cabin.

"Yes. I'll tell you the whole story," Celeste said, leaning over and resting her tired head on his bony shoulder. Not long ago, she'd been hoping to return to the real world. Now, she knew the truth. There was no such thing. There was a thin wall between the rational and the irrational. A wall that could only otherwise be broken by sleep. Now, behind her lids, she could see things she had never seen before that had always been there anyways.

When she opened her eyes and looked toward the dark heavens, she saw the night sky overlap something stranger. A purple sky filled with teeming life. With things that reminded her of prehistoric fossils and of titanic beasts. Things that were there but could not be seen by the human eye.

And I am no longer human, am I?

No.

I've become something more.

Something that resonates with the world beyond and between.

She turned and looked again at Theo, at all the colors of his emotions, his concern. Of the feeble threads of magic he'd clawed at that she'd become enveloped in.

"This is ours," she said.

"What was that?" he asked. He was struggling to focus on the snow-swept road.

She laid a hand over his heart and put her head back on his shoulder. "This is ours. All of it."

He didn't know what to say, but he didn't have to say anything.

She could see Theo's thoughts bubbling up out of him, each fighting for a voice. They were as plain to read as the words in a book, as the great, unblinking eye that hovered just above them, as the tendrils of translucent seaweed that grew downwards from the heavens, as the spears of glass that shot out of the earth and toward the cosmos, connecting this planet to planets lightyears away like ladders without footholds.

She could read his thoughts as clearly and as simply as she could the mind of the shapeshifter that followed cautiously behind the car, certain it could become Celeste's familiar if it asked nicely, if it pleaded for forgiveness.

Celeste hadn't yet decided whether she would grant it such a mercy.

It was something she'd have to consult Bokrug about.

From the shadows surrounding their car, there lurked other things. Horrors beyond description.

Things with names that sounded like shouts of intergalactic rage. Shaggoths and spindly-legged ghouls. Subterranean creatures with beards made from writhing tentacles, each bearing rubbery wings upon their arched backs, each bisected by prickly spines.

These night-things had always been there, even on the drive up the mountain on Friday. But before, Celeste hadn't known how to see them. They'd been there, right in the corners of her eyes, observing her with inhuman expressions, wanting neither harm nor happiness to befall her.

She would speak, someday, to these things. Hear their tales, learn how to pronounce their names, despite the limitations of her tongue. Perhaps, like Bokrug, she could grow more than one. Eventually, she'd know even more languages than Brown Jenkin had, and she'd speak them all fluently.

There was knowledge to pursue. A section of her

brain had been opened after being kept for ages behind a locked door, sealed away because, before this weekend, the terrible truth of it all would have driven her mad.

With Bokrug, she'd learn it all and more. How to conjure great beasts, how to heal any ailment, and how to keep herself young even as the years swam by. She'd outlast Lavinia. Already, she was stronger than the old witch had ever been. It was only up to Celeste now to hone her strength, to understand it, to aim it where it needed to be aimed.

But for the present, all she wanted was sleep.

She wanted, more than anything, to close her eyes and dream of a fantasy called humanity. A dream she'd long ago dreamed and wished to dream again.

Maybe there was a ritual for that too.

Maybe.

I'm thankful you decided to read *Our Sarnath,* and I truly hope you enjoyed it! I say this about most of my books right when they come out, but this is a special one for me. The idea to do a "romantic" retelling of *The Doom That Came to Sarnath* struck me suddenly and came to me almost gift-wrapped. What you read on the page, the visuals, the scares, the relationship between Celeste and Theo, and the ending are *exactly* what I envisioned for this book the day I first came up with it. And I want you to understand how rare this is. When it comes to my writing, nothing tends to ever go according to plan. I'm a notorious "pantser" who tends to reject the idea of outlining, letting my whims and impulses guide the book rather than a strict plot. But lately that, and many of my other habits, has started to change, and *Our Sarnath* is the first big example of that.

It's not the first time I've outlined a book from beginning to end. I've done it many times before.

But it is the first time I followed that outline . . . to the letter.

I don't know what changed or why I felt I had to stick super closely to that initial idea, but I think it came from some anxiety that this idea was too good to divert from.

I didn't want to lose what I initially wanted.

Either way, I'm super happy with how this one turned out. I like the dreamy tone, the chilly atmosphere, and I'm excited to have tackled one of the most underrated Lovecraft stories in this way.

Now, before any scholars get mad at me, I understand that I didn't exactly follow all of Lovecraft's descriptions to the letter. In the original story, the people of Ib are voiceless, with bulging eyes. Also, I messed around some with the whole Taran-Ish idea (in the original story, Taran-Ish was the high-priest of Sarnath rather than a worshiper of Bokrug). I'm very much aware that I'm taking creative liberties and that some people are Lovecraft purists and won't be pleased with these little changes I made. But . . . that's the joy of interpretation. If I told Lovecraft's story exactly the same way he did, then there wouldn't really be a point in retelling (or remaking) it, would there?

What I wanted to get right about Lovecraft was the weighty sense of dread one experiences when faced with the unexplainable, and the academic tussling between the sleeping and waking worlds. I wanted to write, as well, a book that explains the process of encountering a cosmic horror that drives smart people toward insanity.

A lot of people think they're writing a "Lovecraftian" horror story when, really, their only exposure to his work has been through the Stuart Gordon movies. And while I *love* and *adore* those awesome, awesome films, we have to remember that Gordon is Gordon . . . and Lovecraft is Lovecraft.

His stories weren't about sex and tentacles and over-the-top splatter. They were about beholding things that man should not behold. About looking old gods and ancient history in their wet eyeballs and screaming in response to their thundering voices. His stories were about cults and witchcraft and devout worshipers, and about unnamable atrocities lurking in the dark corners of libraries and cemeteries.

I also wanted to write another queer book with *Our Sarnath*. The more repressive our current climate becomes, the gayer my books are.

In this one, I wanted to focus on how hard it is for queer folk to claim our own queerness when that part of us has been repeatedly, systematically, and spiritually suppressed.

There's a *lot* of childhood trauma between the lead characters, with Celeste's mother having beaten her for being gay and Theo's neighbor sexually abusing him and grooming him into her disturbing religious practices. I wanted to write about how people with trauma can heal themselves, and each other, but I also didn't want to sugarcoat it. Healing doesn't happen overnight just because a therapist said the right words or you found the perfect relationship that "fixed" you. It takes effort and time and involves a lot of painful transformations and reckonings. After I was abused, I spent years not even acknowledging it to myself. It festered deep inside, then reared its ugly head up right when I thought I was "past it." My journey has been a rocky one, and that's the journey Celeste and Theo end up taking in *Our Sarnath*. Even though I've never written my personal story exactly out in a book, the feelings these characters feel ring true for me.

Our Sarnath is not autobiographical. People always assume when I write about surviving abuse that it's exactly true-to-life and I'm really writing down what happened to me in detail. No. All my books are fictional. Even the close-to-life ones, like *Psych Ward Blues.* I like to distance my real story from my fictional ones as much as I can.

In real life, my mother is a supportive and sweethearted woman and I was never lured into Satanic practices by a neighbor . . . I was actually abused by people my age, who took advantage of my trusting nature.

I put my raw emotions into Celeste and Theo anyways, had them battle their unique traumas with some of the same terror and confusion I've felt (and still feel to this day).

That makes *Our Sarnath* personal for me.

Not that it mirrors my real life, but that my life informed how the characters think in a dark situation.

As I've made clear already . . . I'm super happy with this book. I can only hope readers will like it the way I do, but at the end of the day, this is one of those times where I wrote what *I* wanted to read, and I'm confident there's an audience out there for that.

Anyways, I'm doing two more "cabin" books. This is kind of the start of a trilogy. You won't have to read these books in order, but I'm very interested in writing about isolated environments and different couples taking part in "rituals." *Our Sarnath* will be the only Lovecraftian one from the three. You'll just have to wait and see what the next book will be about.

While you wait on that, I have a bunch of finished books I'm hoping to release next year, and I've outlined the third and final *Summer Never Ends* slasher! That'll be a hoot!

I've made it pretty clear on Facebook that I'm totally done with extreme horror and am having more fun writing weirder stuff, so if that's what you're into . . . you'll be eating well in 2026!

Until then, I wish you the best on your next journey . . .

And I hope you have pleasant dreams.

From Utah, with love
Judith Sonnet
10/9/25

Judith Sonnet is a trans woman who grew up in Missouri and now lives in Salt Lake City, Utah, where she collects vintage books, movies, and Halloween decorations. Her favorite authors are Ray Bradbury, H.P. Lovecraft, Charles L. Grant, Richard Laymon, and James Joyce. Her favorite movies are *Carnival of Souls, The House by the Cemetery, It Came From Outer Space,* and *Girl's School Screamers*. She believes in UFOs and Bigfoot.

Other MHP books by Judith Sonnet

The Home
Torture the Sinners!
Low Blasphemy
Coming soon: No One Rides for Free

More From Madness Heart Press

Squirming All the Way Up
Ten Words for a Wicked Woman
PINS
Bound with Briars
Blade Job
Curse of the Ratman
Lights Out
Pure Hate
The Bighead
The Television
Trip Chainsaw
Whispers of the Dead Saint
Kennel
Thrust Into Battle
Czech Extreme
The Reattachment
ALL MEN ARE TRASH

www.ingramcontent.com/pod-product-compliance
Lightning Source LLC
Chambersburg PA
CBHW030918060726
47591CB00005B/1589